I parked the ~~wheel~~ ... ~~worn by~~ ... e stack was fairly low at the end where I was. As I grabbed an armful, I noticed the other end of the pile had collapsed backward onto the ground. It hadn't been visible from where I left the wheelbarrow.

"Darn it." I went to investigate. We wouldn't want the wood on the ground where it would get damp, especially at this time of year when the weather was iffy and it was six days between clambakes. When I bent to retrieve a log I saw it. The edge of a heavy boot sticking out under the collapsed portion of the pile.

"Sonny, come here right now!"

I thought he might protest, but my voice must have conveyed my urgency. He was by my side in seconds. Silently, I pointed to the boot.

"It's Jason!" Sonny shouted. As soon as he said it, I recognized the boot. We both scrambled to remove logs, Sonny frantically digging his way toward Jason. When the logs were cleared, Sonny bent over him. "Jason, buddy, Jason!"

It was clear to me, and seconds later clear to Sonny, that Jason was dead. . . .

Books by Barbara Ross

Maine Clambake Mysteries
CLAMMED UP

BOILED OVER

MUSSELED OUT

FOGGED INN

ICED UNDER

STOWED AWAY

STEAMED OPEN

SEALED OFF

EGGNOG MURDER
(with Leslie Meier and Lee Hollis)

YULE LOG MURDER
(with Leslie Meier and Lee Hollis)

HAUNTED HOUSE MURDER
(with Leslie Meier and Lee Hollis)

Jane Darrowfield Mysteries
JANE DARROWFIELD,
PROFESSIONAL BUSYBODY

Published by Kensington Publishing Corporation

SEALED OFF

Barbara Ross

KENSINGTON BOOKS
KENSINGTON PUBLISHING CORP.

www.kensingtonbooks.com

KENSINGTON BOOKS are published by

Kensington Publishing Corp.
119 West 40th Street
New York, NY 10018

All Kensington titles, imprints, and distributed lines are available at special quantity discounts for bulk purchases for sales promotion, premiums, fund-raising, educational, or institutional use.

Special book excerpts or customized printings can also be created to fit specific needs. For details, write or phone the office of the Kensington Sales Manager: Attn.: Sales Department. Kensington Publishing Corp., 119 West 40th Street, New York, NY 10018. Phone: 1-800-221-2647.

Kensington and the K logo Reg. U.S. Pat. & TM Off.

First Printing: January 2020
ISBN-13: 978-1-4967-1795-5
ISBN-10: 1-4967-1795-3

ISBN-13: 978-1-4967-1798-6 (eBook)
ISBN-10: 1-4967-1798-8 (eBook)

33614081578659

This book is dedicated to my new granddaughter,
Etta Ann Donius,
our happy cutie with the best baby laugh evah

Chapter One

"He has to go." My brother-in-law, Sonny, brought his face, which was flushed bright red behind his freckles, down to mine. He was mad. I knew why he was mad. And he was probably right. Which made *me* mad.

"Has something new happened?"

"Look!" Sonny stepped back and pointed dramatically toward the roaring hardwood fire that heated the rocks we used to cook the food we served at our authentic Maine clambakes. The fall afternoon sun glinted off his short red hair, causing me to notice for the first time that it was thinning.

From the great lawn on Morrow Island where we stood, I followed his finger to the bit of shoreline where the fire burned. A familiar scene was playing out. Jason Caraway, a longtime member of Sonny's fire pit crew, leaned on a rake and flirted madly with Emmy Bailey, one of our servers. At forty-five, Jason was more than a dozen years older than Emmy, but he was handsome and well muscled from hard physical labor, which he performed both here at the clambake and on his lobster boat. His abundant dark hair showed some gray and there were laugh lines around his blue eyes, which only made him more attractive. Most of all, he had that thing, that pheromone thing that only a few people have, which makes them attractive like shiny objects. You couldn't not look at him.

Emmy smiled, laughed, and stood a little too close. She had tables to set up, lemonade and ice tea pitchers to fill, and caddies of condiments and cutlery to put out to get ready to serve the customers who had arrived on our tour boat fifteen minutes earlier. But she didn't move. It was easy to see why men were attracted to Emmy. She had a cute round face surrounded by curly blond hair and she was curvy in all the right places. But more than that, there was something about her that was solid, in her body—the way it seemed to grow out of the ground, like a tree—and in her personality. She was a busy single mom who worked two jobs to keep her little family afloat in the trailer she had parked on her grandmother's property. She'd been dealt a tough hand, which she'd compounded with some bad decisions of her own when she'd been younger, but she didn't let it get to her.

Beside me Sonny said, "Here we go."

As we watched, Pru Caraway, Jason's ex-wife, strode down to the fire from our kitchen carrying a basket of scrubbed, skin-on potatoes wrapped in foil to be cooked with the lobsters, steamed clams, and other foods that made up the clambake meal. She stepped in between Jason and Emmy, even though there was barely two feet for her to squeeze into, and handed the basket to Jason.

He thanked her for the potatoes, put the basket down, and stepped closer to Emmy, forcing Pru out of the circle. Pru didn't move and instead talked directly to

Jason, clearly scolding him for something. I couldn't hear her from where we stood, but I doubted that mattered. The point of her speech wasn't to convey information. It was to get Jason's attention and keep it off Emmy.

I'd seen variations on this dance since July, when Jason had started flirting with Emmy. Both he and Pru were valued longtime employees of the Snowden Family Clambake Company. The whole awkward dynamic hadn't been so visible when the clambake was in full swing. But since Labor Day, we'd been open only for one seating each on Saturdays and Sundays and for special bookings like corporate picnics or bus tours during the week. The teachers who had worked with us all summer had returned to their school districts, the college students to their campuses. We were holding the clambake together with a skeleton crew, and that upped the tension created by having two formerly married people and the current person of interest for one of them working on the same small island.

"Now watch," Sonny muttered. Terry Durand approached the little circle, carrying an armload of hardwood. It was a lame excuse to intrude. The fire didn't need more wood. The clambake fire crew, Jason, Terry, and Sonny, would soon be removing the wood embers with their rakes, leaving only the hot stones behind. The food—two lobsters, soft-shell clams called steamers, a potato, an ear of corn, an onion, and an egg for each guest—would be covered with seaweed and salt-water-soaked cotton tarps and cooked by the hot rocks below it.

As Sonny and I watched, Jason looked Terry in the eye and said something dismissive, following his words with a sharp shake of his head. Terry dropped the wood and stood his ground, his chest pushed out. Emmy backed up a step, as if she was uncomfortable and wanted to move away. Jason put a hand on her forearm, urging her to stay. Pru stayed where she was, a raw red hand on her thin hip. The tension floated up from the group like a dust storm, visible and uncomfortable.

"Pru's the aggressor," I pointed out. "It's her behavior that's changed." Pru had made her displeasure with Jason's attention to Emmy known to everyone, though she'd never started something with the two of them directly before. Never scolded Jason publicly as she was clearly doing now.

"Terry's what's different," Sonny countered. "Besides, we're not firing Jason or Pru. They've worked for us forever. They worked for your dad, for Pete's sake."

As if to prove Sonny's point, Terry moved in tighter, standing directly in front of Jason in the space Emmy had created when she'd backed up. He was too close, and clearly none of the four of them were happy.

Around them, all over beautiful Morrow Island, smiling guests played bocce and volleyball, hiked over the high hill to the little beach, or simply relaxed at the picnic tables with friends and family while they enjoyed a drink and anticipated the feast. It was a gorgeous Saturday, the first weekend in October. The sky was cloudless, the sun bright, the temperature nearly perfect. Earlier in the week, there'd been a vicious three-day storm, the remnant of a hurricane, which had kept the lobster boats in the harbor. Sonny and I had come out to the island afterward to clear away the downed branches and right the blown over furniture. All and all, the island had come through pretty well.

"You see what I mean?" Sonny pointed to Terry. "We do hot, dangerous work at the clambake fire. I can't have all this going on. I need my guys focused. I need to be focused, not wondering if a fistfight is going to break out."

I couldn't deny what he said, so I tried buying time. "Two weeks, Sonny. Six clambakes. Today, tomorrow, and the cruise ship special on Monday, and then three days over Columbus Day weekend. Then we'll be shut down for the season. This"—I gestured toward the group of four below us—"will get worked out over the winter. Emmy will either be with Jason or Terry or with neither of them. If she's with Jason, Pru will have learned to live with it. If it's not sorted out by the spring, I won't ask Terry back."

"I want him gone today."

Sonny knew what he was asking of me. Terry was the older brother of my boyfriend, Chris Durand. They had been estranged for years. That had finally ended in early August when Chris visited him at the Maine State Prison in Warren. Terry had been there for ten years for a convenience store robbery during which a clerk had been shot.

Terry had been released in late August after serving his full term. He was jobless and homeless and had returned to Busman's Harbor, where we all lived and where he'd grown up. He was living on Chris's old wooden sailboat, the *Dark Lady*.

Chris had asked me to give Terry a job. The Snowden Family Clambake was always desperate for help in the fall. Terry had no food service experience and the third guy who worked in the summers with Sonny and Jason had returned to his teaching job in Maryland. The fire pit crew was the obvious place.

Since I'd stepped in to rescue the Snowden Family Clambake from almost certain bankruptcy two years earlier, I had largely kept the peace with Sonny by staying out of his area of expertise, the clambake fire. He did the hiring, he ran his crew. Hiring was rare in any case, since the same guys returned year after year. Sonny put a lot of stock in the group's esprit de corps, and given the mess it would cause if the food wasn't cooked properly, and how dangerous working around the fire was, I could see his point.

So I ran the business, and worked the front of the house. Sonny worked the fire pit, and my sister, Livvie, Sonny's wife, along with Pru and one other longtime employee, put out the rest of the clambake meal—the chowder, melted butter, clam broth for cleaning the clams, and the blueberry grunt we served with vanilla ice cream for dessert—from our tiny kitchen. As we neared the end of the season the whole situation felt more and more claustrophobic. I was counting the days until we shuttered.

"Two weeks," I said. "Six clambakes, counting today. That's all I'm asking. You know Terry isn't just an employee."

Sonny puffed his barrel chest out. "Jason isn't just an employee, either. Neither is Pru."

"Neither is Emmy." Emmy was the mother of Sonny's daughter's best friend, among other things.

It was true. None of them were just employees. "Please," I finally said.

Sonny shrugged his broad shoulders and gave up. "Okay. But it's a mistake. When this blows up, and it will, I'm going to say I told you so."

"Fair warning," I agreed, and we each returned to our predinner duties.

Twenty minutes after dessert was served, I rang the ship's bell, mounted on a post at the entrance to the dock, giving guests a ten-minute warning to pack up their stuff and climb aboard our tour boat, the *Jacquie II*. Emmy Bailey put her son Luther in his stroller to wheel him to the boat. He yelled, "No!" something he was increasingly prone to, and held his body rigid, refusing to bend to fit in the seat.

"Luther, please," Emmy murmured. "Mommy's tired." Luther relented.

Terry appeared out of nowhere. He picked up Luther's diaper bag and whistled to Emmy's eleven-year-old daughter Vanessa, who was nearby, running in circles with my niece Page. Much as I wanted the clambake season to end, I didn't want the girls' golden summer to. But they were back in school. The days were shorter, the nights chilly. One down and five more clambakes to go.

I was in charge of getting Page back to the mainland. As soon as the main course had been served, Sonny had taken Livvie back to town in our Boston Whaler. We were having a special dinner at Mom's house that night and Livvie was cooking.

Pru and Jason had also caught a ride with them, as they often did when their duties at the clambake were done. Over the last two summers, Jason had occasionally arrived at the island in his gleaming new lobster boat. The *Money Honey* was top-of-the-line, a gorgeous boat with a powerful engine and all the gizmos a lobsterman could want. He hadn't brought it today. He'd come and gone in the Whaler. Pru usually commuted that way,

too, since her work in the kitchen required her to start
before the *Jacquie II* arrived.

Vanessa and Page responded to Terry's whistle and
headed for the boat, running and giggling.

"Slow down, girls!" I called. "Watch out for the guests."
Page and Vanessa shuffled to a stop and joined the back
of the line for boarding. Terry, the diaper bag slung over
his shoulder, helped Emmy push Luther to the top of the
path that led to the dock.

While the clambake guests slowly made their way
aboard, I turned and sprinted in the other direction, up
to the top of the island to the abandoned mansion built
by my mother's ancestors. Windsholme. Since the last
Morrow had stayed there in 1929, the once-grand house
had been given just enough maintenance to keep it
standing. Two summers before, during my first season
back home running the clambake, the mansion had
burned. Not burned down, but its winding central staircase was destroyed as were parts of the roof. Now, after
much debate, and a huge stroke of not-so-blind luck, my
family was renovating it.

The original plan had called for the demo crew not to
work on the few remaining days when the clambake was
open. They had another job going on the mainland
where they could work those days. But losing three
days to the storm had thrown everything out of whack.
Mark Cochran, the general contractor, had called and
begged. We all hoped to have the demo done by the time
the weather turned, when work on the island would be
too difficult to continue.

Mark opened the French doors that led from the
dining room as I stepped onto the front porch.

"Mark!"

"Julia." He didn't look particularly happy to see me.

He folded his flannel-clad arms, hugging his clipboard to his chest.

"I wanted to make sure you're doing demolition on the third floor only. You haven't done anything on the second or first, right?"

He grimaced, impatient with my checking and rechecking. "We've removed the fire damage around the staircase as agreed and now we're working on the third floor. Also as agreed. Don't worry, Julia. The first and second floors are intact."

I tried to get around him to step inside, but he planted his size-thirteen work boots firmly in my path. "Don't you have a boat to catch?" He looked down toward the dock where the line of passengers waiting to board had dwindled to a handful.

"It's just that, as I told you, my mother's"—I searched for the word to describe the relationship—"elderly cousin is coming to the clambake tomorrow. She's the only person alive who stayed in the house in its glory days. I would be crushed if she couldn't see it before we ripped out walls and pantries, and—" I struggled, the words gone. After a long, circular journey, I had come around to the idea of updating the mansion for a business and family with twenty-first-century needs. Even though I'd never lived there, I'd roamed its empty rooms since I was a child. If I was having trouble with the destruction that had to come before the construction, I couldn't imagine how Cousin Marguerite would react.

"So you've told me." Mark shifted from foot to foot in his work boots. "The crew and I have to get back to town. It's quitting time."

I nodded my thanks and turned to go. Mark's regular carpenters had done some preparatory work, but the demo crew had only been able to spend one day at the mansion. The previous week's storm had come as something of a surprise. It had been expected to track much farther to the east and pass "safely out to sea" as the forecasters loved to say, forgetting about all the people in peril out there. By the time it turned, Mark had to rush out to the island with his regular employees to secure Windsholme and cart away the debris the demo crew had created in their single day of work so it wouldn't fly around and cause more damage. He had job sites all up and down the Maine coast. We'd been lucky he got to us in time.

As I climbed off the porch I looked over at the two dumpsters parked by the house. One was partially filled with fire-damaged wood, the other with molding and plaster covered in pieces of wallpaper I recognized as coming from the servants' rooms on the third floor. The demo crew was making great progress in the right places.

Captain George let out one long, loud blast of the *Jacquie II*'s horn and I raced down the path toward the boat. I reached it just in time.

Right after we pulled away from the dock, a wave of chatter ran through the boat. Page and I followed it to the stern where the guests stood smiling, pointing, and taking photos. A young harbor seal sat on a rock at the end of the island, in front of an empty osprey nest. The seal had big, round, intelligent eyes, like a dog's, with whom he shared a common ancestor.

"So cute!" Even Page, who'd seen seals all her life, was impressed.

The young seal sat up straight, staring forward, ready for the cameras.

I watched until I lost sight of him in the gathering dusk.

When we'd seen the last guest off the *Jacquie II*, Page and I took off for my mother's house at a run. Mom was expecting some very special guests. I'd promised to be there. I'd promised to help. In other words, I'd made all sorts of promises I couldn't keep. I was barely going to make it before the guests arrived.

"Beat you!" Page reached Mom's house fifty feet ahead of me. At eleven, she was almost my height. She had her dad's fiery red hair and freckles and her mother's long legs and swimmer's body. I couldn't see myself winning a foot race against her ever again.

Page scurried into the house, but I was still on the big front porch when my boyfriend Chris's taxi pulled to the curb. The cab was one of Chris's three jobs. In the summer he kept busy late at night ferrying tourists back to their hotels from the restaurants and bars. In the off-season, the fares consisted mostly of taking elderly clients to the supermarket and hairdresser. He wasn't on the meter now. He'd met the train from Boston at the station in Portland and then driven the hour and a half to Busman's Harbor.

Chris jumped out of the cab and ran around to the passenger side to open the door. He offered his hand to the woman inside. Tiny and frail with great age, she didn't refuse his help, something she might have done a year before.

"Thank you," my mother's distant cousin, Marguerite, gasped. Then she spotted me. "Julia! How lovely to see you. Thank you so much for sending your young man to meet us at the train."

"I was happy to do it, Mrs. Morales," Chris said.

"Marguerite," she insisted. "I am not going to tell you again."

"Marguerite." Chris yielded to her command, as any sane human would.

A young woman with wild blond hair, black at the roots, emerged from the other side of the backseat. I ran to greet her. "Tallulah! How was the trip?"

Tallulah Spencer looked pointedly at her grandmother. "Challenging. I'm glad we did it this year."

"I hear you," I reassured her. "We'll try to take things as easy as possible."

"Good luck with that." Tallulah flashed a smile and hugged me.

By that time, my mother and sister, Livvie, were on the porch stairs, calling out greetings. Chris pulled an old-fashioned suitcase and a modern rolly-bag out of the cab's trunk.

"Jacqueline, what a fine old house," Marguerite said to my mother. She looked up toward the cupola on the mansard roof. "I remember this house well. You can see it from anywhere in the harbor. When I was a child, it meant we were coming to town from Morrow Island for a special treat."

"I hope it comes to mean something just as happy to you on this visit," Mom said. "Let's go inside."

Marguerite came up the walk, stomping her cane with her right hand while holding onto Chris's arm with her left. Tallulah fluttered behind, fussing. Livvie and I picked up the suitcases from the sidewalk and followed.

Inside, the house smelled of my sister Livvie's delicious cooking. My nephew, Jack, eight months old, sat in a rolling gizmo. He was the type of kid who was never still for long, and he'd learned to turn that thing into a weapon. I looked at it, and then at Marguerite's ancient, skinny legs, and shivered.

Marguerite had no such qualms. "The youngest!" She greeted Jack. "I cannot tell you how happy it makes me to see the family go on."

"Me too." Mom patted Marguerite's shoulder. "Come into the living room and make yourselves at home. Do you need to freshen up?"

Chris helped Marguerite out of her camel hair coat. She wore a beige cardigan underneath, over a black dress. Her white hair, like always, was in braids pinned to her head, framing her olive-skinned face, sharp nose, and hooded brown eyes.

Tallulah slipped out of her cropped leather jacket. She had on a sleeveless dress that showed off the tattoo of a flowering branch that started on her back and flowed over her right shoulder onto her breast where a songbird perched, ready to sing. Tallulah was a singer, her husband Jake, a jazz pianist. They'd graduated from Emerson College in Boston in the spring and she'd taken off on a summer tour of small clubs. Now she was back in Boston auditioning and doing open mike nights, looking for the next gig. The couple's lives in the arts were greatly supported by their ability to live rent-free in Marguerite's town house in Boston's Back Bay.

Tallulah had worn a sleeveless dress every time I'd ever seen her, only covered by a coat when she went outside in the depths of winter. She seemed to have an internal heat source the rest of us lacked. I wondered whether her leather jacket had been a concession to the fall weather, or to her grandmother's views about what constituted appropriate dress for train travel.

I snuck upstairs to the hall bathroom, ran a clean washcloth over my face and a brush through my hair, trying to make myself presentable at the end of an already long day. The face that looked back at me in the mirror was my mother's. I'd always argued everyone said I looked like her for superficial reasons. We were both small and blond. But in recent years some weird aging thing was happening to me and our features had become more similar. I was conflicted about it. My mom was lovely, but she was also, well, my mom.

I headed down the back stairs to the kitchen where Livvie was stirring rice in a pot on the stove.

"Where's Sonny?" I asked.

Livvie cocked her head toward the back door. "Grill."

"What are we eating?"

"Greek lamb chops."

"Yum. How can I help?"

"Set the table?"

I did a mental count. Mom, Marguerite, Tallulah, Chris, Page, Livvie, Jack, Sonny, me. "So eight, plus the high chair. I'll need to put in two extra leaves."

"Get Page to help you. Good china, Mom said."

"Roger that. Page!"

Page and I put the leaves in the dining room table and I set her to work on the placemats, napkins, and silver. I went to the corner cabinet and counted out eight china plates and seven crystal wineglasses. Mom's mother had died when she was young and the wineglasses, silver, and china were among the few Morrow family things that had been passed down to her. She always took pride in them, but they were particularly special today because they had been at Windsholme when it was a grand summer house, and Marguerite had been there, too.

As we worked, I listened to the talk that floated in from the living room, so far pleasantries about the train trip.

"I'm so sorry Vivian couldn't make it," Mom said. Vivian was Marguerite's daughter and Tallulah's mother. Mom was polite to her backbone and I had trouble believing she was truly sorry. Marguerite and Tallulah were lovely, but in their branch of the family charm was evidently a generation-skipping characteristic. Vivian was selfish, vain, and grasping, with a near constant need to be flattered. Every one of us had been glad when it turned out Vivian couldn't come. Not that my mother would ever say such a thing.

"And Jake," Mom said. "We're so sorry to miss him." Tallulah's husband Jake was a lovely man, a stabilizing influence on his impulsive wife, but he'd been unable to leave Massachusetts for this trip.

"Yes, it's too bad," Marguerite agreed. "I would have liked to show Vivian and Jake Windsholme. But as it is, Tallulah will be their eyes and ears. She'll take plenty of photos and videos." Through the archway I watched Marguerite, who sat upright in one of the high-backed chairs, using her cane to punctuate her words. "I'm grateful I get to see Windsholme one last time. I never thought I would."

Livvie came through the dining room door. "Good. Everyone's here. Let's eat."

We piled around the table. Livvie served the lamb chops while Chris poured wine. I put Jack in his high chair and scattered Cheerios across the plastic tray.

When we were all seated, Mom raised her glass. "To Windsholme," she said.

"Windsholme," we all repeated.

Livvie's lamb chops were, as always, beautifully seasoned and perfectly cooked. She served them with a simple rice dish and a salad. For a moment we were all silent, enjoying the food.

"Delicious," Marguerite said. "Now tell me about your plans."

The plans, along with Marguerite's great age, were the reason for the urgency of having her visit now, even though the ocean was cold and the October weather iffy.

Windsholme had sat empty on Morrow Island since the Depression. More recent generations spent their summers on the island in the little house by the dock. The mansion had been deteriorating for years. I couldn't remember any time in my life when its future hadn't been debated. It would be expensive to tear it down and haul all that trash off the island, and even more expensive, many times more expensive, to fix it up. So for decades no decision had been made.

Then, over the previous winter, my mother had discovered a family she'd never known she had, including Marguerite, Vivian, and Tallulah, and she had come into a fortune she'd never guessed she was entitled to. Fortune was perhaps too strong a word, but enough to renovate Windsholme. A lot of money.

Mom spoke up. "Yes. The plans. We have them here, actual floor plans for the renovation, if you'd like to see them."

Marguerite shook her head. "Not yet, I think, thank you. I remember Windsholme the way a child does, disconnected rooms, flashes of wallpaper, my mother's dressing table, a corner of a rug on which I sat. I want to tour the house tomorrow to remind myself, before I look at your changes."

"Yes, of course," Mom said. "Julia, what's the plan?"

"We'll take the *Jacquie II* out for the clambake. I'd love Marguerite and Tallulah to experience it. Wyatt Jayne, the architect, will meet us on the island and give us all a tour of the house." I turned to Marguerite. "How does that sound?"

"Lovely," Marguerite answered. "It couldn't be more lovely."

Chapter Two

I was at the bow of the *Jacquie II* the next morning as we neared Morrow Island. Chris, Mom, Marguerite, and Tallulah were on board as well. Marguerite had insisted on sitting outside on the upper deck, even though the weather had turned overnight and the day was cool and gray. Tallulah had wrapped her grandmother in blankets and the two of them sat with Mom as she and Marguerite chatted about her summers on the island.

Chris came up behind me.

"Thanks for taking the day off to help," I said.

"Happy to do it." He flashed me a smile, which made him even more handsome. With his tousled brown hair, green eyes, and the dimple in his chin, Chris attracted a lot of attention. He was tall, and his body had been shaped by the hard physical work he performed for his landscaping business, his primary job, which he supplemented with the cab and working as a bouncer at Crowley's, Busman's Harbor's most touristy bar.

"Look, do you see him there?" I pointed toward the outcropping of rocks where our island ended. The young harbor seal was there, exactly where I'd seen him the day before. "Why is he by himself?"

"Because he's old enough. His mom let him know it was time to leave her," Chris answered.

"They usually haul out in groups. He looks lonely."

"You're anthropomorphizing."

"Easy for you to say."

Chris laughed.

Captain George made an announcement about the seal over the loudspeaker system and soon the bow was full of people excitedly taking photos with their phones. The seal posed like a celebrity showing off a designer-labeled frock and then capped off his performance by diving into the frigid water.

"Time to think about going south with the rest of your clan," Chris called to him as he swam past us.

"Like a snowbird," I said.

"Except he's only going as far south as Massachusetts or Long Island," Chris responded.

"Then like a summer person."

Wyatt Jayne met us at the dock on Morrow Island. I'd asked her to give Marguerite and Tallulah the tour of Windsholme not just because she was the architect over-seeing the renovation, but also because she was an expert on the history of the house and its original archi-tect, Henry Gilbert.

"Wyatt, I'd like you to meet—"

"Marguerite Morales!" Wyatt threw her arms around Marguerite. "Née Morrow. The last living person on the earth to have seen Windsholme in its original state."

"I'm not sure I like it put that way." Marguerite seemed taken aback and I held my breath, but then she smiled. "I am she."

"I cannot wait for you to tell me everything about the house," Wyatt enthused.

"I was going to say the same to you," Marguerite responded.

"But first," Mom said, "we eat."

"We'll take it from here." Chris offered Marguerite his arm. Mom and I ran off to our clambake jobs, she to the gift shop and me to my hosting duties.

Sonny was hard at work at the clambake fire. He, Livvie, Page, and Jack had come out to the island earlier on the Whaler along with Pru and our third cook, Kathy Cippoli, and Jason and Terry, who needed to arrive in time to get the fire started. I wondered if it had been tense on the little boat. A number of guests stopped in their progress up the walk toward the dining pavilion to observe the clambake operation and ask questions. Jason and Terry worked in apparent harmony, at least for the moment.

I helped guests pick out dining tables, most in the semi-sheltered dining pavilion due to the less than stellar weather. Emmy made sure her tables were ready, putting out the caddies that contained the utensils and the paper towel rolls that served as napkins and filling pitchers with drinks.

The old boat the demo crew used pulled up at the dock. They were off to a late start, perhaps because it was Sunday. Six men disembarked and headed for Windsholme. I would have preferred they not work on the day we gave Marguerite her tour. Seeing Windsholme after all this time was bound to be emotional for her, and to see people tearing it apart . . . I couldn't imagine. But Mark Cochran had insisted they had to work due to the time lost to the storm, and I'd reluctantly agreed.

"Remember, only the third floor," I called to the crew

chief as he walked by me. He nodded, so at least he'd heard me.

The crew chief was in his fifties, a fireplug of a man with a bald head ringed by graying hair. The next three men, who walked by me in a clump, looked as you'd expect a demo crew to look, all broad shoulders and bulging muscles. Next, some distance back, came a skinny guy with a prominent Adam's apple, who looked like he was barely out of his teens. Mark Cochran had told me the men were all Russian immigrants who went from town to town and only did demolition work. He had used them before and spoke of them highly. He said we were lucky they were available.

The last man to come up the path was a handsome guy in his thirties. He was dressed in the same coveralls as the other men, but something about him was different. I watched him for a moment, wondering what it was. He wasn't quite as big as the three big guys, but that wasn't it. It was something about the way he moved, his walk.

I turned my head slightly and realized I wasn't the only one watching him. As he walked toward the clambake fire, Jason stared straight at him. He caught the man's eye and both of them started. It looked like they had recognized one another.

I couldn't imagine how Jason and a member of a traveling Russian demo crew knew each other. The day before had been the only one when the clambake had run and the crew was on the island at the same time, and the demo crew had arrived before the clambake employees did and had stayed on after. Maybe the two of them had run into one another in our public restrooms or something like that. But the look I'd seen pass between them appeared to have more significance.

I wandered to our little gift shop to check in with

Mom. In the fall she divided her time between Linens and Pantries, the big box store in Topsham where she was assistant manager, and the clambake. She'd worked in Topsham the day before and then had gone home to prepare for Marguerite and Tallulah's arrival. I'd handled the gift shop as best I could, along with my hosting duties.

"Did you sell a lot of the lobster cookies yesterday?" Mom asked.

We fed people more than enough during the clambake, but the gift shop carried lobster-shaped sandwich cookies, red velvet with vanilla cream, which people purchased as souvenirs.

"I may have sold maybe two packages," I answered. "I'm sorry I didn't write it down."

"My inventory is off by more than two dozen. Have you all been eating them behind my back?"

"I wasn't able to be in the shop as much as I wanted yesterday," I said. "You better check with Page and Vanessa."

I left Mom and went to ring the ship's bell to indicate the first course was served. When the guests were seated the waitstaff delivered the creamy clam chowder, perfect on this chilly day. Mom put a CLOSED sign up in the gift shop and met me at the picnic table where Marguerite sat with Tallulah, Chris, and Wyatt. I didn't normally eat the clambake meal. I was too busy with work, but we didn't normally have a ninety-six-year-old who'd once lived in Windsholme visiting, so I made an exception.

"We'll tour the house as soon as we finish eating the main course. That should allow enough time for us to go back to the harbor on the *Jacquie II* with the rest of the guests," I said.

"Fine, fine," Marguerite agreed. For someone who'd

traveled such a long way, she seemed in no hurry to visit the house.

We headed to Windsholme as soon as we finished our lobsters. When we started the steep climb from the dining pavilion to the house, I momentarily regretted not renting a wheelchair for Marguerite. But she took the hill like a champ, thumping her cane along the path with Chris on one side and Mom on the other.

Wyatt led the way, her long brown hair blowing in the cool breeze. She was dressed in a neat, rust-colored shirtdress, accessorized by a perfectly tied scarf in fall colors and a pair of flats that matched the dress. A stranger might have assumed the professional-looking outfit was because she was giving an important client and her honored guests a tour of a major project, but I knew better. Wyatt had always dressed beautifully, even when we were in prep school. We'd lost track of each other for years before she'd turned up to work on the renovation. Her careful dress and grooming hadn't changed in all those years.

"The house, as I'm sure you know, Marguerite, was built in 1890 by your father, Lemuel Morrow, the year after his father, Thomas, the head of the family, died," Wyatt said as we walked. "Windsholme is attributed to the architect Henry Gilbert."

She stopped on the porch that ran the length of the front of the house. "Gilbert was a master. He was entirely self-taught and critical to the development of these Maine coast summer homes. He was meticulous, insisted on being onsite every day when his designs were built. He specified the woodwork, the wallpaper, even the furniture and rugs. It was a time when American architects turned away from the fuss of the Victorian style and embraced the straight lines of our colonial heritage. Gilbert had emigrated from Quebec Province, but he embraced the trend fully and pushed it forward.

"Gilbert could have become a John Calvin Stevens or even the new H. H. Richardson, but he died tragically young. If Windsholme was his first commission, as we believe, there are only five houses built during his lifetime, and a half a dozen others completed from his plans after he died."

Mom, Chris, Tallulah, and I hung back, allowing Marguerite to be the closest to Wyatt.

"We'll start in the dining room," Wyatt announced.

The French doors to the east wing had been left propped open. The main entrance to the house now led to the giant hole the fire had burned in the floor of the great hall, neatly severing the east wing from the west wing. The rooms in the east wing up to the third floor were accessible via the servants' staircase. Getting to the second and third floors in the west wing, the larger part of the house, required climbing scaffolding erected by the workers. That wasn't going to work for Marguerite. I hoped she'd be happy with a full tour of the first floor and a partial tour of the second.

Livvie and Sonny hurried up the hill toward us. Aside from Marguerite and Tallulah, we'd all been in the empty mansion many times, but everyone wanted to tour the place with someone who had lived there in its prime.

"Hello, hello." Mark Cochran came through the French doors onto the porch with his arm extended. "You must be Mrs. Morales." He took one of Marguerite's blue-veined hands into his enormous paw and worked her arm up and down like he was pumping a well. "Mark Cochran, general contractor. So excited to meet you."

Mark was a bear of a man, toweringly tall, heavily muscled, and with an expanding gut. He was dressed in brown cords and an expensive-looking yellow sweater. He looked like a successful, middle-aged version of the former high school football player he had once been.

Like everything else about the day's expedition so far, Marguerite took it in her stride. Withdrawing her hand, she said, "I'm excited as well."

"Shall we begin the tour?" Wyatt asked a little too loudly. She was nervous like the rest of us.

We went through the French doors into the dining room. Fortunately, except for the lingering smell of smoke that still haunted the room on damp days, it was largely intact.

"The murals in the dining room, as you probably know, are attributed to Reynold Ripley," Wyatt said. "There's no signature, but the style is highly recognizable, and we know he worked in the area at the time. Is that what you were told?"

We all looked at Marguerite, hoping she could confirm the story. She didn't respond. She stared at each of the four hand-painted walls in turn, her heavily lidded old eyes wide, her mouth slightly open. Wherever she was, it wasn't here with us in the present day.

Starting in a corner, she put a hand up and traced the outline of the harbor and the schooners at full sail depicted in the mural. She walked past the big stone fireplace, running her hand along its rough face, and then continued with the mural on the other side.

Tallulah videoed it all dutifully, though I wondered in the dim light of the dining room if anything would be visible. The electricity was off for demolition and the gloomy day didn't help, especially since the deep porch prevented much of the outdoor light from filtering through the French doors. All the inside doors to the room were closed, the passageway to the kitchen and back stairs, and the pocket doors to the burned-out great hall. We could hear the far-off thumps and bumps from the demo crew working on the third floor.

We watched in silence as Marguerite made her slow pilgrimage around the room, examining each wall. I could tell Wyatt was bursting with questions, but none of us wanted to break the spell. After she returned to the center of the room, Marguerite pulled her arms into the sleeves of her camel hair coat, literally gathering herself. We stared expectantly.

"It's a shock," she finally said. "It's exactly as I remember it. When I stand here, I am a little girl. The dining room table is there." She pointed to the center of the room. "And I can barely see the top of it. The second maid has come in to lay the fire in the fireplace. I can smell the cooking coming from downstairs and the noise of the cook at work."

As we listened, transfixed, there was a particularly loud thump from the demo workers and I jumped a little. I wasn't the only one.

"May we see the kitchen?" Marguerite asked.

Wyatt smiled. "You remember the way?"

Marguerite smiled back. "Of course."

Chris and Tallulah rushed to either side of her, but Marguerite didn't wait. She used her cane and marched resolutely to the door that led through the butler's pantry, past the entrance to the back stairs, and onto the balcony that surrounded the two-story kitchen.

I hung back and motioned for Mark to do the same. "Can we open up the pocket doors? It's so dark and close in here."

Mark rolled the double doors back, opening the dining room to the great hall. The big windows at the front of the house did lighten the place up considerably, though the window over the remains of the staircase had been lost to the fire and was boarded up. There was yellow caution tape strung around the hole the fire had burned in the floor of the great hall straight through to the basement. I didn't know if it was for our benefit or more likely for the safety of the demo team. Overhead, I caught a glimpse of a catwalk made of scaffolding bridging one side of the second floor to the other.

"We'll be able to take Marguerite to the second-floor rooms in the west wing!" I pointed excitedly. "Thank you so much."

Mark beamed. "I thought you'd be pleased. We were going to need the scaffolding for the demo team anyway, so I had my guys put it up because I knew this visit was important to you. It's why I didn't let you in yesterday. I hoped you'd be surprised."

"Thank you." There was the sound of a sledgehammer and a splinter of wood. "That sounds close. Are you sure they're only working on the third floor?"

"I reminded them this morning."

We caught up to the group on the balcony over the kitchen. It ran around all four sides of the room and was ringed by beautiful mahogany cupboards, glass-fronted for china and glass, drawers for silver, shelves for linens. The cupboards were all intact and I hated the idea that they would soon be demolished. Wyatt had designed a modern caterers' kitchen for the main floor. If the house was intended to allow us to schedule and run events— weddings, corporate meetings, and so on—we wouldn't want to be running up and down stairs for service. It was the twenty-first century, not the nineteenth, and the renovation was for a working family, not one with servants. Still it hurt. I couldn't imagine how Marguerite felt.

Marguerite stood against the rail on the far side of the balcony, looking into the kitchen below. There was nothing down there but an old wooden icebox with its doors off and the hulking wood stove that had been used for cooking throughout the house's occupancy. The linoleum floor, installed during a hasty 1920s renovation, was cracked and curling in places, its original light and dark green pattern barely discernible.

It was clear that wasn't how Marguerite saw the kitchen. "This was my favorite place in the house," she said in a strong voice. "On rainy days when there was little to do on the island, our cook, a lovely old woman named Mrs. Stout, would let me and my brother's children 'help' her. What patience that woman had. Of course, we were no help at all." Marguerite pointed to a corner of the kitchen. "Her rocker used to be right there."

The group, led by Sonny, started to move. This scene of nostalgia for past days of family grandeur wasn't his thing. "Moving on," he said in a loud voice. "You don't want to miss the boat. Upstairs next?"

Mark nodded.

We crowded through the narrow hallway and went up the back stairs one at a time. Chris positioned himself behind Marguerite, waiting on each step while she slowly climbed. At the top, a door brought us into the great hall again, with yellow caution tape ringing the hole where the staircase should have been and the scaffold bridge leading across open space to the west wing.

There was another loud bang.

I hustled everyone into the master bedroom and then pulled Mark to the side. "That sounded like it came from the second floor. Make them stop until after Marguerite leaves."

Mark headed off across the scaffold bridge.

"My mother's dressing table was here," Marguerite said as I returned to the bedroom. "So she could look down the hill, across the great lawn, and to the sea as she got dressed."

I had thought Marguerite might linger in her mother's old room, but she did not. Her memories of the room were not as strong a pull as her memories of the kitchen. She'd led us back into the hall when Mark Cochran hurried across the scaffold bridge, his dark brows pulled together, lips set in a grim line. As soon as he was close, he said, "Julia, Wyatt, can I talk to you?"

We met him where the bridge joined the old hallway floor.

I knew what he was going to tell me. "The demo team *is* working on the second floor," I said.

"No," he said. "They're not, but there's something you need to see."

"Great." I looked over toward the rest of the group, milling outside the master bedroom door. I caught Livvie's eye, held up one finger, letting her know the group should wait, and then followed Mark and Wyatt across the scaffold bridge.

In the east wing of the house the large master suite, with its sitting room, dressing room, bedroom, and bath took up the entirety of the second floor. The west wing was larger and quite different. It had a long hallway, which led past the closed doors of half a dozen family bedrooms. I didn't see any signs of destruction as we passed, and breathed a sigh of relief.

At the end of the long hallway, the single door was ajar and that was clearly where we were headed. The large room beyond it, which stretched from the front to the back of the house, had always been called the nursery. I didn't know if the room had specific significance for Marguerite, but I braced for the destruction I expected to see.

"Oh my!" Wyatt had preceded me into the room. Whatever she was reacting to had to be bad. I steeled myself. But when I entered the big room it was empty, like all the rooms at Windsholme. It was only when I turned fully around back toward the door that I saw Wyatt and Mark staring at a huge gap in the wall.

"What is—?" I didn't get further. Through the still intact wood framing, I saw the room. A perfectly but modestly furnished room, with a single bed with an iron bedstead. The sheets were yellowed, the summer blanket moth eaten, but the bed was made. There was a small wooden bureau, a writing desk with an open notebook on its surface. A nightstand held an oil lamp, a book, and a pair of spectacles. The room looked like someone had walked out its door moments before and would return at any minute.

"What the heck?" I looked from Wyatt to Mark. They both stood openmouthed, as astonished as I was.

The wall separating the room from the nursery had been completely demolished, the rubble cleared away. The remaining framing clearly showed a door frame into the nursery, but there had never been one in my memory. The plaster on the back and sidewalls of the little room was still up and there was no door to the hallway or the room on the other side.

"Did you know this was here?" I asked them.

"No. I thought it was empty space, eaves boxed in." Wyatt pointed toward the outside wall where the only window was high overhead, way above eye level. "I don't think I missed the window. I must have thought it went with the room above."

"What happened here?" I asked Mark.

"Exactly what I'm trying to find out."

He'd no sooner said that than two members of the demo crew entered the room—the short, squat, middle-aged man I recognized as the crew chief and the handsome man who'd exchanged looks with Jason Caraway at the clambake fire. "I told you no work on the second floor," Mark said.

"Not our fault," the crew chief said in heavily accented English. "We did before."

He looked at the other man, who spoke up. "This was the first thing we did on the first day. The scaffolding was in place, so it was easy to reach. It was before you told us to confine our work to the third floor. We were shocked to find this room. Because it was furnished, we finished with that wall, cleaned up, and moved upstairs. I meant to tell you about it, but with the storm I forgot." The man's English was unaccented. His command of the language marked him as a native English speaker.

Mark didn't look happy. We could hear the shuffle of feet and the tap of Marguerite's cane headed toward us. The theme from *Jaws* played in my head. "We'll talk about this later," he said, dismissing the men. They turned and were gone, exchanging muttered "excuse me's" with the group in the long hallway.

Wyatt was inside the hidden room, opening bureau drawers. "This isn't recent, that's for sure. The stuff in here is from the late 1800s, turn of the last century maybe."

"Why was the room sealed up like that?" I asked. "Why was there no door?"

"That is certainly the question," Wyatt agreed.

Livvie came through the nursery doorway followed by the rest. "Sorry, we couldn't wait any longer. If we're going to make it back to the—Holey-moley."

"Yeah," I agreed.

"What is it?" Mom asked.

"It's a room. A room with no door," Wyatt answered. Everyone looked at Marguerite. "Do you remember a room being here?" Wyatt asked her.

Marguerite stared at the place where the wall had been, then slowly shook her head. "No. I'm positive there was nothing there when I was young. I slept in this room with my brothers' children." Her hand swept around the old nursery. "My bed was against that wall." She hugged herself. "It's strange to think all that was behind it the whole time."

"The boat," Livvie reminded us.

I turned to Mark and Wyatt. "I'll see everyone off on the *Jacquie II*," I told them. "Then I'll come back. I'll take the Boston Whaler home with Sonny and Livvie later."

We made our way, slowly, out of the house, the rest of us keeping pace with Marguerite. Once outside, we started down the hill to the great lawn. The *Jacquie II* sounded her horn, letting the guests know it was time to get aboard. The customers gathered their things, found the others in their groups, and started for the boat.

Chris leaned in toward me. "I'll go ahead and let Captain George know we're on our way." I nodded my thanks and he ran down the lawn, avoiding the people strolling on the path toward the dock.

There was a shout from below. People stopped boarding the *Jacquie II*. Faces all turned in the same direction, over toward the clambake fire.

There was another shout, and a scream. Sonny and I took off, following Chris by a hundred paces or so. The knot of people had backed up on the path from the dining pavilion to the dock.

"Excuse me, excuse me." I hurried forward.

"What's happening?" a man asked as I passed him.

"I don't know. Please stay back." I kept moving.

Sonny and I reached the dock and I looked over toward the fire. At first I saw nothing, but then, further down the point, by the giant woodpile where we stored our hardwood, I spotted two figures moving on the ground. Chris had almost reached them.

When we got closer, it became clear what was happening. Terry had Jason on the hard-packed dirt and was pounding him. The sound was even worse than the sight. I'd never heard anything quite like it in my life. Off to one side, Emmy cowered, protesting. "Stop. Please stop." Her words had no effect.

Chris dove for his brother, knocking him off Jason. As they tumbled apart Terry was still slugging. "Enough!" Chris commanded. Terry was the older brother, but Chris was in control. Terry stopped punching.

Sonny and I went to Jason, who was still on the ground. His nose was bloodied, his left eye already swelling.

"You okay, buddy?" Sonny reached out a hand. "Can you get up?"

Jason lay there for a long minute during which I wondered if we'd have to call the Coast Guard to have him evacuated. "I'm okay. I'm okay," he finally said. "Give me a minute."

"You did this! You did this!" I hadn't noticed Pru coming up behind us. She was red in the face, spitting fire. I followed her hand to where she was pointing. It wasn't pointing at Terry. She was pointing at Emmy, who stood frozen, in tears.

Chapter Three

It took a while to get things sorted out. I sent Chris and Terry home with Mom, Marguerite, and Tallulah on the *Jacquie II*. After the action was over, the crowd resumed boarding. Chris hustled Terry up to the bridge so he wouldn't be sitting among the guests, reminding them of what they'd seen.

Sonny agreed to take Jason and Pru back to the harbor in our Boston Whaler, and then to return to pick up Livvie, their kids, Wyatt, and me. Jason was up and walking around. He vehemently declared he had no interest in going to the police station (Pru's suggestion) or to the hospital (everyone else's).

Emmy was another problem. It didn't seem right to send her and her kids home with either Jason and Pru or on the same boat as Terry. Since Livvie, Page, and Jack were staying on the island until Sonny returned, we decided Emmy and her family should, too.

"I'll look after her," Livvie volunteered.

As we walked toward the dock, Sonny sidled up to me. "You have to fire Terry. Today."

"I know," I said.

"If you don't, I will."

"No. It's my responsibility. It will be better coming from me."

Sonny put a hand on my shoulder. "It's tough. I get that he's your boyfriend's brother."

I was touched. Sonny didn't show sympathy easily or often, especially not to me. "Thank you. I got us into this. I'll get us out of it."

He grunted and we went our separate ways, he toward the Whaler and me back to Windsholme.

"What took you so long?" Wyatt, who'd been at Windsholme the whole time, had no idea what had happened.

"Long story. Where's Mark?"

"Talking to the demo guys. They're packing up for the day. Come in here." She beckoned me into the hidden room. "You have to see this. This place is amazing."

I stepped through the doorway in the framing. "Any hints about what happened here, why it's closed up?"

"Not specifically about that, but plenty of hints about who lived here. It's obviously the nanny's or governess's room. Its door opened into the nursery where she could keep an eye on her charges."

"So we know what the occupant did."

"More than that." Wyatt's eyes twinkled. "We know who she *was*." Wyatt picked the notebook up from the writing desk. "It's her journal." Wyatt could barely contain her glee. "We'll learn so much about what the household was like when she was here."

"Which was when?"

"The entry on the first page dated June 4, 1898."

"And the last?" I was dying to know who the woman was, why she'd left, where she'd gone, and, most important, why her room had been closed up with all her things in it.

"This notebook is full," Wyatt answered. "The last page ends in the middle of a sentence on August 8, 1898."

She handed me the journal. It was all in sepia tones, the ink faded to the color of weak tea and the paper darkened to beige. The handwriting was readable, just, a lovely, spidery script that curved across the page.

"Look at this!" Wyatt opened the top drawer. She pulled out a corset, a petticoat, and a pair of bloomers. "There are more," she said. "And look here." The second drawer held two white cotton nightgowns. Wyatt pulled another item out of the drawer.

"What is that?" I asked.

"Bathing costume." She laughed as it unfolded. It had a top with naval insignia on the lapels, a tight waist and knee-length skirt, and there were matching bloomers to go underneath.

"What is that made of? It looks so heavy. I would sink straight to the bottom in that thing."

"Serge." Wyatt rubbed the fabric between her thumb and forefinger. "Twill cotton with ridges on both sides."

"I don't know what to do with all of this. Maybe we should get the historical society out here. Offer them the full contents."

"Whatever you do, do it soon," Wyatt said. "The demo guys will have to get to this if we're going to finish this fall." She took out her fancy measuring device with the laser beam. "Meanwhile, I know what I need to do. Redraw the plans. This extra room is in your apartment."

We were in the part of the house that was slated to become part of my summer residence. "Okay," I said.

"You measure. I'll keep poking around until Sonny gets here."

"You go ahead when he gets here. I'll go back with Mark."

I went to the writing desk and sat on the hard, wooden chair in front of it. It was a simple desk with a writing surface, prettily turned legs, and two small drawers. I opened each in turn. There was a pencil in the top drawer that had somehow survived being frozen every winter and thawed out every spring for a century and a quarter. Windsholme had never been heated. The Morrows wouldn't have considered spending time there except in the summer months.

I moved around the room, careful to stay out of Wyatt's way as she measured and jotted notes on her phone. There was a white blouse with long sleeves and puffy shoulders hanging in the wardrobe along with a long skirt. I lifted it out to examine its elaborate construction. It was heavy in my hand and the waistband was impossibly small. Even with the corset, the wearer must have been very slender. The front panel of the skirt was flat, but a series of flared panels in the back would have made it quite full, especially when it was worn over the petticoat. The woman who had owned it was medium height, at least by today's standards.

"Those clothes look more like a governess's than a nanny's," Wyatt said, looking over her shoulder at the skirt. "A nanny would have worn a uniform. A governess would have had a different position, might even have taken her meals with the family, especially in an informal summer house."

"It's weird enough that the room was all sealed up," I said.

"Definitely," Wyatt responded.

"But also, she left everything here, even her glasses, her undies, everything."

Wyatt looked at me, the measuring device clutched in her fist. "I think she died. That's why she didn't take her stuff, and that's why they sealed the room up."

"An extreme reaction."

She was already back to her measuring. "I agree."

"And if you were going to turn the bedroom of a deceased person into a shrine," I said, "wouldn't it more likely be a family member, a child maybe?"

"It's not a shrine if no one can visit it," Wyatt pointed out. "Sealing the room made it more likely forgotten than remembered."

"Maybe someone was sick here and they sealed the room up to keep the disease from spreading." I'd picked up the journal and felt the urge to drop it, then laughed at myself. No germs could survive over a century of Maine winters in an unheated house.

There didn't seem to be much more to say. The late afternoon light barely filtered into the room. "I'm going to take the journal to Marguerite," I said. "Perhaps it will jog her memory. Not about something she experienced, since 1898 was long before she was born, but maybe something she overheard the adults discussing."

Wyatt nodded. "It's a long shot, but we might as well take advantage of her being here."

I put the journal in the Snowden Family Clambake tote I used as a handbag and walked to the dock where our Boston Whaler was tied up. Sonny was back. He waved as he passed by with a wheelbarrow piled with boxes of liquor. In the summer, Sonny, Livvie, and their kids lived in the little house next to the dock, but once school started for Page, they moved back to their house on the mainland. That meant the island was empty overnight, and all week long during this late part of the season. So we took some minor precautions like locking up all the booze in the little house, though anyone even mildly determined could have broken in.

Emmy Bailey sat on a bench by the dock watching Vanessa and Page fooling around. If they'd been scared or upset by the fight, neither showed it. They stood over the cages where the live lobsters were stored for the next day, pointing and giggling. Emmy's son, Luther, was already strapped into his stroller, and she moved it back and forth, comforting him.

"Careful, girls," Emmy said, a reflexive comment, not because of any immediate danger.

"Sure, Mom," Vanessa answered.

I sat down next to Emmy. "Are you okay?"

She sighed. "I am. Upset mostly. I was never in danger of being hit."

"I get that. It was between Jason and Terry."

"But it was about *me*."

I didn't say anything right away, hoping she would go on. When she didn't I asked, "Yes, but *what* is it about you?"

Emmy sighed, a long, drawn-out sigh. "I thought you might know."

"I might know a little."

She glanced around quickly to make sure the girls were out of earshot. "I've been seeing Jason outside work."

That didn't surprise me. "Pru doesn't like it much," I said.

"No, she doesn't. They've been divorced for five years. And it is awkward with the three of us working here, but I thought we'd been handling it pretty well. Pru's in the kitchen, I'm on the tables, and Jason's working the fire, so it's not like we're in each other's faces all day." She paused. "What do you think, Julia? Have we been out of line?"

I thought back through the last couple of months. Jason had been flirting with Emmy almost since she started working with us. But he was a flirty guy. Almost any interaction between him and a young woman, myself included, looked like flirting. He also flirted with older women, certainly with my mom. And with men. He was a chronic flirt. I thought his intent was to flatter, to communicate, "You're interesting." But he also wanted to bring the reflected glow back on himself. Jason wanted to be liked.

So Jason's flirtations with Emmy weren't that big a deal, especially since, as she said, they had limited contact when they were working, and Emmy seemed to welcome them.

Family meal was another matter. During the busy part of the season when we ran two seatings a day, after the lunch guests left and before the dinner guests arrived, the employees ate together. In our tiny kitchen Livvie, Pru, and Kathy put out something fresh, filling, and inexpensive as a part of their duties.

At family meal Jason had sat across from Emmy exclusively for most of the summer. Pru sat as close to them as she could. As a cook, she would be among the last to find a seat. From wherever she was seated, she interrupted with insults and irrelevancies, lobbed at the top of her voice. The other employees caught on, and took up as many seats close to Emmy and Jason as they could fill, not out of any particular allegiance to either of them, but because eating a meal in the middle of someone else's family spat was never pleasant. This did not deter Pru, however, who only got louder.

It wasn't great, but it was limited, and pretty well managed by the group.

"No, you weren't out of line," I said. "I would have said something if you were. If anything, Pru was."

"And she's been here forever." Emmy's eyes swept around the dock, surveying the girls, checking on Luther in the stroller. She was a good mother.

It was true, I supposed, that Pru's status as a longtime employee was the reason neither Livvie nor I had spoken to her. That and the fact that she was more than a decade older than us. But mostly, I'd figured it was between the three of them. It was slightly uncomfortable for the rest of us, but it was their business and, during the summer, I'd believed they would work it out.

"But then Terry started work here," Emmy said.

"Terry made it more complicated," I acknowledged.

"He's a nice guy," Emmy said. "He helps me with things like packing up to leave at the end of the day or getting the kids into my car at night. It doesn't . . . I never . . . he never. And it's not like with Chris."

With that elliptical sentence she'd said a whole ton. Fortunately, or unfortunately, I had the background to decode it. When Emmy said Terry wasn't like Chris, she was referring to a miserable conversation she and I had much earlier in the summer. Chris was absolutely convinced his brother Terry was Vanessa's father. His only evidence was Vanessa's green, green eyes, so like his own. Chris swore she was the spitting image of his mother.

Emmy, for her part, was unclear on Vanessa's origins. She'd been born before Emmy had married her ex-husband, who was Luther's father. Vanessa was the product, Emmy had told me, of an alcohol and drug-fueled one-night stand with a man she could not re-member. That behavior was in her past, and aside from Vanessa, there was no part of it Emmy wanted to recall.

Emmy had noticed Chris had an interest in Vanessa, and had misunderstood it. She and I had a deeply morti-fying conversation where she had asked me to tell my creepy boyfriend to back off.

Chris had been horrified by her fears. He'd immedi-ately backed way off. I convinced him that if there was anything to his theory, it was between Terry and Emmy. He agreed, mostly. But there was one more terrible revelation hanging over the whole situation. Chris's mother had Huntington's disease. If Terry had inherited the gene, if he'd passed it to Vanessa, didn't Emmy have a right to know? And Vanessa when she was old enough?

Chris's revelation to me about his mother's genetic disease and his father's reaction to it had answered many of my questions about him, but had raised many new ones. Like Terry, he'd never been tested for the repeating sequence of genes that caused Huntington's devastat-ing symptoms. With no treatment and no cure, he saw no reason to be tested.

"I don't want to live my life differently," he'd said. "We all die. I don't want to know how I'm going to die, just like everyone else. Besides, I could be hit by a bus tomorrow."

Given the number of gigantic touring buses rumbling through Busman's Harbor's narrow streets during foliage season, it wasn't an impossible scenario.

But him opening up about the disease and his refusal to be tested left open the question of our future and the possibility of children. Chris had lived with the knowledge about his mother's disease and its effect on his family for more than two decades. I'd had two months to adjust to it. While he was always patient about my many questions, I tried not to bring it up all that often.

When Terry got out of prison, Chris told him about Vanessa. Chris had told me so, but I would have known regardless because of the way Terry acted around Emmy and her kids. It wasn't intrusive or overly familiar, but there was a wary watchfulness there if you knew what to look for, a helpfulness that went beyond collegiality.

And that was where the situation had stalled out. I didn't know for sure that Terry hadn't talked to Emmy, but there was no indication in their interactions that he had. I wondered what Emmy really thought about him hanging around.

I wanted to ask her about him, but that question would have led back into territory that I'd told Chris was none of our business. So I sat with her in silence on the bench, watching the sun get lower in the sky, and waited for the others to be ready to return home.

Chapter Four

On the mainland I stopped at Mom's house on the way to my apartment to get cleaned up. Chris was already in Mom's kitchen cooking. He'd volunteered to feed the family that night. He and Livvie had a friendly cooking rivalry going and the rest of us were the beneficiaries.

I thought Marguerite might be napping after the physical and emotional exertions of the day, but she and Tallulah were in the living room, both reading in the two easy chairs that faced the sofa.

Mom entered the darkening room with a bottle of wine tucked under her arm and cheese and crackers on a wooden cutting board. "You all look so serious. It's time for a break. Hello, Julia. I didn't know you were here." She put the wine bottle and the cheese on the coffee table.

"I'm not. I have to run home to take a shower."

Mom went to the dining room to fetch wineglasses and I followed.

"How are you doing?" she asked in a low voice.

"Okay. I guess. I have to fire Terry."

"I know." She handed me two glasses. "I'm sorry."

"I wanted it to last until we shut down for the season, so we could all get out of it gracefully. It will be hard for him to find a job as an ex-con."

"It would have been hard anyway. And he would have been looking for a new job no matter what. You did your best."

"I guess."

"You did, Julia."

We returned to the living room. I reached into my tote bag and pulled out the journal. "Wyatt and I found this in the sealed room. We thought you might want to look through it, Marguerite. The dates are way before you were born, but maybe some of the names will be familiar."

Tallulah reached out to take the book. "Cool! Maybe we can figure out what happened, Granny."

"When you're done with it," I said, "you can help us decide whether we donate it to the historical society, or if it's some precious family heirloom we should keep."

Tallulah had already opened the book to the cover page. "Lilly Smythe, 1898," she said.

"Thank you, Julia, for giving me a new mystery to solve at my age," Marguerite said, though I had the feeling if anyone did any solving, it would be Tallulah.

When I got back to Mom's everyone was there.

"Almost dinner," Chris said, offering his cheek for a kiss. The food smells were fantastic. "Can you and Page get the table again?"

"Of course. Page!"

Page and I got to work. This time I put china soup

bowls on top of the dinner plates and added bread plates to the place settings. I helped Page find the soupspoons and she put one at each place. I got the silver candlesticks out and lit the candles. Then I took a porcelain tureen to the kitchen and filled it with hot water to warm it. "We'll serve the cioppino from this," I told Chris.

He raised an eyebrow. Normally at my mother's house soup or stew would be served from the pot it was cooked in. "Will the queen be dining with us tonight?"

"Pretty nearly," I answered, and he laughed.

We gathered around the table. Mom had invited our across-the-street neighbors, Fiona and Viola Snugg, known to all as Fee and Vee. She thought Marguerite and Tallulah would find them delightful, which, of course, they did.

Chris dished out the meal, his own version of cioppino, the Italian-American fish stew invented in San Francisco. Chris used typically East Coast seafood, instead of West Coast. He started his broth with lobster bodies, something we always had plenty of on hand.

When the bowls were dished out, I leaned over mine and let the steam hit my face. Mom picked up her spoon. "Let's eat."

The cioppino was delicious. The different tastes and textures of the shrimp, clams, lobster, haddock, and Maine crab shone through, even as they blended perfectly with the tomato base.

"A triumph," Vee pronounced. She was the third cook in the triumvirate with Livvie and Chris. He beamed.

The conversation flowed around the table. We interrupted and talked over one another as we told Fee and Vee about the secret room at Windsholme, eager to give our differing experiences of the event. They were both properly impressed.

When she finished her meal, Marguerite said, "Tallulah and I have been reading the governess's journal."

We all demanded to know what they'd learned.

"We've only read the first entry. Would you like to hear it?" Marguerite asked. "Tallulah, dear, why don't you bring it here?"

Tallulah left and returned with the journal and Marguerite's reading glasses.

"The entries start in June of 1898," Marguerite said as she opened the book. "Lilly Smythe is a young woman who's come with the Morrow family to Windsholme." She pronounced it "Sm-eye-th," with a long "I."

I worried the candlelight in the room would make it impossible for Marguerite to see the faded script, but she put on the wire-framed glasses and read in a voice that was stronger than any person her age had a right to. Nonetheless, we all leaned in to hear her, hanging on the words.

> *"June 4, 1898*
>
> *"I arrived at the appointed time at the town house in the Back Bay. Two carriages were waiting to take us to the sailing yacht in Boston Harbor. I sat with the young men whom I had only met for a few moments when I had my interview. William is fourteen and Charles eleven. I am to tutor them this summer before they go off to school in the fall. Their father, Mr. Lemuel Morrow, is particularly concerned they are deficient in German and mathematics."*

"She was a governess to my brothers," Marguerite explained to Fee and Vee.

This brought an inevitable round of questions and explanations. How could Marguerite, living and breathing today, have brothers who were adolescents in 1898?

The answer was a trick of our family history. Lemuel Morrow had fathered William and Charles when he was in his twenties. As a widower, he had married a much younger woman when he was sixty and they had produced Marguerite. Thus, Marguerite had a father, my great-great-great grandfather, who was born on the eve of the Civil War. It seemed amazing, but it was also true.

The candlelight glimmered and danced, adding to the atmosphere. It was like we were back in time, when these very candlesticks had sat on the long dining table at Windsholme. Marguerite picked up the journal again and continued reading.

> *"When we got to the docks there was another cart piled with steamer trunks three deep. I had only my valise, with a second blouse and skirt, two nightgowns, my undergarments, and a bathing costume I borrowed from my cousin Bertha.*
>
> *"Before I knew it, we were on the Morrow yacht, preparing to leave. The party is large. There is Mr. and Mrs. Morrow and their boys. Mr. Morrow's mother is with us, too. She is almost as wide as she is tall and wears a perpetual scowl. I hope I won't have much intercourse with her. Then there is Mr. Morrow's brother, a bachelor, quite a bit younger than Mr. Morrow, I think. I am to call him Mr. Frederick.*
>
> *"And that's just the family! We have a cook and two maids traveling with us, along with the*

*yacht captain and four crew. I am told the yacht
will return to Boston from time to time to bring
weekend parties of guests to the island. In
addition to those on the boat, there will be a
gardener and a porter awaiting us there, and a
housekeeper who has gone ahead to open the
mansion with help from two local women. This is
the largest and grandest household I have ever
worked in. I hope I am up to the task."*

Marguerite stopped reading. We all looked at her expectantly.

"But that doesn't tell us why the room was sealed up,
or why her things were still there," Livvie said. "Have
you skimmed ahead?"

"You are as impatient as your cousin here." Marguerite tipped her head toward Tallulah. "Some things
must be savored. Besides, you are going to want to hear
this next bit."

I grabbed my empty bowl along with Marguerite's,
which she'd pushed forward to make room to hold the
journal in front of her. Others jumped in to help. I
brought out the dessert, apple pie contributed by Vee,
and served it along with vanilla ice cream and coffee.
They all groaned about how they couldn't eat another
bite, but no one turned down a piece.

When everyone was served, Mom said, "What is it
we absolutely need to hear, Marguerite?"

Marguerite put her glasses on and read.

*"The yacht was finally loaded and we left in
the late afternoon. A light supper of cheeses and
meats was served on the deck and we all made*

*merry, singing and playing guessing games. All
except the cook, Mrs. Stout, who was sick despite
the calm seas and took to her bunk."*

"Mrs. Stout!" I almost shouted. "Wasn't that the name
of the cook you told us about today?"

Marguerite smiled, pleased I remembered. "She was
indeed. I remember her as an old woman in the late
1920s. She would have been so much younger when
Lilly Smythe knew her."

"Did she ever tell you any stories about a governess
or a sealed-off room?" Vee asked.

"No, but I was quite young. Maybe too young for the
story, whatever it was. Mrs. Stout worked for my half
brother William and his family, who lived in New York
City. They didn't approve of my mother and we never
visited them there. I saw Mrs. Stout only in the summers
at Windsholme."

Marguerite turned a page of the journal and continued.

*"My young charges are delightful! I look
forward to working with them. On the deck,
young Charles approached me, staring deeply.
'You are too beautiful to be our governess,' he
whispered.*

"'If it wasn't for her specs,' William added.

*"'Charles! William!' Mrs. Morrow senior
scolded. 'You apologize to Miss Smythe.'*

*"'I don't see why Charles should apologize,'
Mr. Frederick responded. 'He speaks the truth.
We have our own Gibson girl among us.'*

*"I blushed and old Mrs. Morrow snapped,
'Enough. All of you.'*

*"The stars at sea are the brightest I have ever
seen. Finally, we all made for bed. I slept in a
compartment filled with bunks for the female
servants.*

*"In the morning, we were at anchor. When I
came up on the deck, Morrow Island was before
us. The house they call Windsholme sits at the
highest point on the island. It has a deep porch
where I believe I will spend many happy hours.
It looks strong and sheltering, ready to protect
those who live inside. What a grand adventure is
in store. I believe this will be the happiest
summer of my life."*

Marguerite closed the journal. There'd been a sharp,
collective intake of breath when Marguerite read the
name "Windsholme." We knew Lilly Smythe had been
there. That's where we'd found the journal, but her love
of the house wove her more tightly to us.

Sonny stood. "It's a school night." Page had crept off
during the reading to play in the living room. The normally active Jack dozed in his high chair. While Livvie
gathered up their things, Sonny pulled me aside. "Did
you fire Terry?"

"First thing in the morning, I promise."

"We'll walk out with you," Vee said to Livvie. "Thank
you for a lovely evening."

Chris and I stayed to clean up. "The journal passage
was so idyllic," I said as he washed and I dried. "Imagine
the days when the family arrived on the island in a sailing yacht."

"Yes," he said. "Imagine you spent the summer trim-
ming their hedges, making their meals, and boiling their
laundry. If you were lucky."

"Let me dream," I pleaded. "It's going to be the happiest summer of her life."

"Honey, the only reason you have that journal is because that woman's room was sealed up like an Egyptian tomb. How can you imagine her story has a happy ending?"

Later, as we walked home, I told Chris I had to let Terry go.

"I know. I was there," he said. "When?"

"I'll go over to the *Dark Lady* first thing in the morning."

Terry, so recently out of prison, couldn't afford a cell phone. In some ways, I was grateful. It would be easier to look into his eyes when I spoke to him than to imagine his reaction if I did it over the phone.

Chapter Five

But when I got to the *Dark Lady*'s berth in the morning, the boat wasn't there. The wooden sailboat was Chris's pride and joy, inherited from an uncle. Terry had been living aboard since he'd been out of prison. The water in the harbor got colder every day. The cabin was cramped and uncomfortable. In a couple of weeks, as soon as the snowbirds who were renting Chris's cabin headed south, Terry would move out there.

I stood for a moment, staring through the clear water where the boat should have been to the stony harbor bottom. Terry had Chris's blessing to live aboard, but did that include taking the *Dark Lady* for a spin? I scanned the harbor looking for her familiar sail but didn't see it.

Maybe Terry had taken the sailboat out to Morrow Island to report for work. He'd never done that before. He always went over with Sonny and the others in the Boston Whaler. But there was always a first time. Maybe he didn't want to ride with Jason after their fight. What if I'd missed him? Sonny would be furious.

I left the marina and walked to the concrete town pier

where our ticket kiosk stood and our tour boat was tied up. Sonny and Livvie were already aboard the Boston Whaler. Jack and Page were with Mom. She'd bring them over later on the *Jacquie II*. Sonny fussed with the Whaler's engine and grumbled.

"Hey!" I called to get his attention.

"Julia. To what do we owe the honor?"

"I went to the *Dark Lady* to let Terry go, but he wasn't there. I came down here to head him off in case he shows up."

Sonny looked around, hand to brow, exaggeratedly scanning the harbor. "Nope, not here."

"Very funny. I'll stay in case he shows up."

"He's not the only one who isn't here."

What Sonny said was true. Now that Sonny and Livvie were living back on the mainland, they took the Whaler out to Morrow Island every morning with the two cooks who worked with Livvie in the kitchen, Pru and Kathy Cippoli, and the two guys who worked the clambake fire with Sonny, Jason, and for the last four weeks, Terry. The rest of the employees followed later, catching a ride on the *Jacquie II*, but this group had to get a head start or the food wouldn't be served on time.

"At least today it's a cruise ship," I said. One of the small cruise lines that visited our harbor during foliage season had contracted with us to provide a harbor tour and serve lunch to their passengers. A hundred and two people had signed up, half our usual number of guests. Plus, the cruise started in Nova Scotia, so by the time they got to Busman's Harbor, they would be used to being on time and queuing up. Groups from a single tour were generally easier to manage.

"I guess," Sonny said. While the smaller number of

guests would make it easier on the waitstaff, it would make only a marginal difference for Sonny at the clambake fire.

"I'm here! I'm here." Kathy, the third cook, who worked with Livvie and Pru in the kitchen, ran up the pier. "Sorry, I'm late."

"Thank goodness." Livvie hugged her once she'd climbed aboard. "I was beginning to worry I'd be cooking alone."

"I'm going to be alone," Sonny grumbled. "No Jason, and no Terry."

"You didn't want Terry," I protested.

"Well, he doesn't know that, does he?"

"I'll come," I said. "I'll come now and help." Sonny's red eyebrows were pinched together over his nose. The work at the clambake fire was hot and heavy. Clearly he didn't think I was capable. "I can't help you during the bake, but I can help you set up," I added.

He rolled his big shoulders. "No call from Pru?"

Livvie looked at her phone and shook her head.

"Okay, let's go." Sonny started the Whaler while I climbed aboard. "Jason may even be on the island," he shouted over the engine noise. "Sometimes when he takes the *Money Honey* out he forgets to tell me."

Sonny pulled away from the pier and eased us into the harbor. He observed the speed limit in the no wake zone, and then opened her up once we cleared it. At that point, conversation became impossible. I sat back to enjoy the ride.

Jason's fancy lobster boat, the *Money Honey*, wasn't at the dock on Morrow Island when we arrived. Neither were the *Dark Lady* and Terry. I wished I'd called Chris and told him the boat wasn't at its mooring when we were back in the harbor and still had cell service. The old junker Mark Cochran had found for the demo crew was there, and I could see the men moving around up by Windsholme and hear the pounding of sledgehammers and the crash of debris as they threw it in the dumpster.

Livvie and Kathy went off to the kitchen while Sonny and I got to work at the fire pit. We grabbed rakes and pulled out the ashes and charred bits of wood from the previous day's fire. Once the ashes were removed, we repiled the stones that would heat the food for the clambake. The rocks had to be a very particular size, bigger than a brick but smaller than a cinderblock. A too big rock was hard to move and wouldn't heat through easily. A too small rock could get too hot and explode. Sonny had a collection of treasured stones he used over and over. Whenever we were at the beach or in shallow water, all of us kept an eye out for a perfect one. If I found one the right size and it passed Sonny's detailed inspection for composition and density and made it into the collection, my heart swelled with pride. If one of his rocks did break after countless fires, Sonny reacted as if he'd lost an old friend. "That's an old reliable," he would say. "Thank you for your service." Then he would drop the pieces off the dock, returning it to spend its days with its similarly broken brethren.

"Why do you think Jason didn't show up?" I asked.

"He got beat up yesterday, didn't he? Probably he's too achy to work and he looks terrible. Probably he didn't want to see Terry."

"But wouldn't Jason call you if he wasn't coming?"

"I'm sure he figured I'd know why he wasn't here. Why do you think Terry didn't show up?"

"Probably he knew I was going to fire him and thought

he'd save me the trouble." I turned to Sonny. "I'm sorry I didn't take care of that yesterday. Then you could have let Jason know Terry was out and you might not be here alone."

Sonny nodded, focused on piling the rocks perfectly so they would heat up and cook the food correctly.

"I'll start on the wood," I said.

"Julia—" Sonny squinted at me skeptically.

"I'll use the wheelbarrow," I assured him.

I found the wheelbarrow up by the little house and pushed toward the woodpile. The path dipped down by the clambake fire and then climbed slightly upward again toward the flat spot where the wood was stored. I stopped along the way and looked out over the North Atlantic. It was a cool, sunny, fall day with a lovely breeze. The island was peaceful this early in the day with only the four of us—plus the demo crew—working. When the renovation of Windsholme was completed, I would live on the island during the season and get to experience these beautiful mornings.

I parked the wheelbarrow at the woodpile. The stack was fairly low at the end where I was. As I grabbed an armful, I noticed the other end of the pile had collapsed backward onto the ground. It hadn't been visible from where I left the wheelbarrow.

"Darn it." I went to investigate. We wouldn't want the wood on the ground where it would get damp, especially at this time of year when the weather was iffy and it was six days between clambakes. When I bent to retrieve a log I saw it. The edge of a heavy boot sticking out under the collapsed portion of the pile.

"Sonny, come here right now!"

I thought he might protest, but my voice must have

conveyed my urgency. He was by my side in seconds. Silently, I pointed to the boot.

"It's Jason!" As soon as Sonny said the name, I recognized the boot. We both scrambled to remove logs, Sonny frantically digging his way toward Jason. When the logs were cleared, Sonny bent over him. "Jason, buddy, Jason!"

It was clear to me, and seconds later clear to Sonny, that Jason was dead. He lay on his back with his eyes wide open, and the top of his head bashed in.

Chapter Six

Sonny stayed with Jason's body while I ran to the little house by the dock. There was no cell service on the island, but we did have a radio. I connected with Melanie Truitt, the college student who worked in our ticket kiosk.

"Melanie! Listen carefully. I need you to do several things for me."

"Ready." Melanie was a good kid, efficient and not inclined to freak-outs. I was grateful she was on the job.

"I need you to call the Busman's Harbor Police Department on the 911 line. Tell them there's been a body found on Morrow Island and we need someone out here right away."

"A body. Is it someone—"

I used my firmest voice. "Let's not get into that over the radio. Please do as I ask. Then, I need you to call the director of excursions at the cruise line in Jacksonville, Florida, and cancel today's tour. She'll be easier to reach than the ship and she can inform them." I read the director's number off my phone. "Tell her an emergency came up on the island; don't say you've called the police.

Then, offer the passengers a tour of the harbor on the *Jacquie II* and a ride back to town for lunch. Call around to restaurants that are still open. I doubt anyone can take them all, so you'll have to split them up.

"Call Mom to help you. She has Livvie's kids with her, but she can probably come down to the booth with them. She'll know who to call about lunch. The woman from the cruise line may have ideas, too, when you call her." I waited, giving Melanie time to absorb what I'd said. "Have you got that? Police first."

"Yes, Julia. Are you sure you don't want the Coast Guard?"

If someone had been badly hurt or gravely ill, the Coast Guard would have arrived with the needed know-how most quickly. But Jason was beyond their help. "I'm sure. Just the police," I answered.

I went up to the kitchen off the dining pavilion to tell Livvie and Kathy what had happened. After I finished, they were shaken and nearly speechless. I told them to wait there. The police wouldn't want people tramping all over the place. Then I returned to the woodpile to wait with Sonny.

Sonny had adjourned to a tree stump where he sat, studiously not looking at Jason. I joined him there.

"Do you think Jason came out to work early and the woodpile fell on him?" I asked. My mind raced from the downright awful—Pru and Jason's young teenagers getting the news—to the practical—accident on the island, insurance, liability, mess—and then back again.

Sonny cracked the huge knuckles on his right hand. "No way for us to know, right? Did his head get bashed in when the wood fell on him or before? Anyway, if he came out to work early, how'd he get here? Where's his boat?"

Where indeed. That would be something for the cops to figure out.

We didn't have to wait long. In the way of small towns, we knew the first two officers to arrive. Jamie Dawes was a neighbor and childhood friend of Livvie's and mine. His partner Pete Howland was a buddy of Sonny's. They arrived in the harbormaster's boat in less than twenty minutes. While the tourists took a lovely, long boat ride that included islands, lighthouses, seals, and eagles, if you skipped all that you could reach the island quickly.

"We're over here!" I called to the officers as they got off the boat. By that time, Livvie and Kathy had come out of the kitchen. They stood on the deck of the dining pavilion, watching everything going on below.

"Where is this body?" Jamie wasn't the skinny, long-blond-haired, dark-eyelashed boy I'd grown up with anymore. His body and voice exuded authority.

Sonny and I walked to the woodpile with them. Sonny pointed to the body. "There."

"Do you know who it is?" Jamie asked.

"Jason Caraway," Sonny and Officer Howland answered simultaneously.

"You know him?" Jamie turned to Howland.

"Yup." Howland was short and round, his brown hair buzzed so close his scalp showed through. He and tall, slim Jamie were a study in contrasts.

Jamie felt for a pulse, an action I guessed was a formality. He straightened up. "We called the state police Major Crime Unit before we left the harbor to put them on notice. I need to use your radio to confirm we need them. Who's on the island now?"

"Us, Livvie and Kathy Cippoli up at the kitchen. And the demo crew working up at Windsholme."

"I want you all to wait in the little house by the dock," Jamie said to us. Then he turned to Howland. "Tell Livvie and Kathy to go to the house and then go up to Windsholme and collect the demo crew."

Jamie, Sonny, and I trod back along the path toward the little house. Jamie made his radio call and left us. Livvie and Kathy arrived, breathless, moments later.

"They told us to wait here. What do you think happened to Jason?"

Sonny laid it out, telling them we weren't sure if Jason's death was accidental, the local police were bringing in Major Crime, and so on. By the time he was done, the demo crew arrived, five men strong and all speaking Russian, one over the other.

The thin young man I'd noticed the day before approached our group. "Can you tell us what is happening?" The boss stood next to him. The others hung back.

"This morning Sonny and I"—I pointed to my brother-in-law—"found a dead man under the woodpile."

The young Russian translated what I'd said for the men behind him. The group fired questions back at our translator at a rapid pace.

"Did you know this man who died?" he asked. He didn't have the same command of the language as the handsome man we'd spoken to the day before, who was clearly a native English speaker. I couldn't tell if the young man's hesitations were due to lack of knowledge of the language or lack of confidence.

"He was a worker here at the clambake," I said. "What time did you get to the island?"

"We got here at about eight. I am Alex, by the way."

"Was there anyone on the island when you arrived?" I asked. "Was there a boat at the dock?"

He shook his head. "No one."

"Did you see anyone after that?"

He translated. The men shook their heads.

I had a million more questions, but I held back. The state police probably wouldn't be happy I'd asked the ones I had. But there was one I couldn't hold off on. "There was another man with you yesterday. Brown hair, very tan, American accent." The one I'd seen exchange a look with Jason as the crew passed by.

"Dmitri," Alex said. "He wasn't at our place when I woke up this morning. He didn't show up at our boat. We waited. He did not come, so we left without him. That's why we were a little bit late getting here."

They'd waited at their boat for Dmitri. We'd waited at our Boston Whaler for Jason, Pru, and Terry. Like the demo crew, we'd given up and come to the island.

Tragically, Jason was here. Where were the others?

The little house had been closed up for the season, so there was no food or drink inside except for the liquor in the pile of boxes Sonny had left there the night before. Serving that seemed like a terrible idea, so when Officer Howland reappeared Livvie persuaded him to accompany her up to the clambake kitchen where they grabbed a coffee urn, coffee, milk, sugar, and a pan of the blueberry grunt that had just finished baking when the police arrived.

By the time the coffee was made and distributed, a Maine Marine Patrol boat pulled up to the dock. A group of official-looking people disembarked, a medical examiner and crime scene techs, I guessed. Jamie, who'd been keeping watch by the woodpile, strode down to the dock to meet them. Through a window I scanned the crowd looking for two familiar faces.

Finally I saw them, almost the last ones off the boat, Lieutenant Jerry Binder and Sergeant Tom Flynn, detectives with the Major Crime Unit that covered the middle part of Maine. I had known both of them for a couple of years, ever since a body was found hanging from the grand staircase at Windsholme. Over time, they'd grown to trust me and I'd grown to trust them. I was glad they were on the case.

The group from the boat, along with Jamie, clustered around Lieutenant Binder, leaning in to listen to whatever he was saying, nodding their heads in comprehension. When the group broke up, most of them headed in the direction of the woodpile. Jamie came toward us.

"The lieutenant has asked me to set up a place for interviews," he said when he entered. "Where can we do this?" He looked around.

We were gathered in the single room on the main floor of the house. The Russians sat around the dining table in front of the picture window that framed a view of the Atlantic Ocean that went to the horizon. Sonny, Livvie, Kathy, and I were in the living area, Livvie and Sonny on the couch, Kathy and I in the armchairs facing them.

"They should use the dining pavilion," I said. "There's more room. We can go up for our interviews as we're called."

"I agree." Jamie pulled a small notebook from his pocket. "I need everyone's names." He knew the four of us. Alex, the young translator, helped him spell the Russian names.

I followed Jamie out the door and pulled him aside. "Do you know if they're looking for any more bodies?"

Jamie's dark eyebrows rose. "Should they be?"

"This morning, four people who were expected on

this island never showed up. Jason, Terry Durand, Pru Caraway, and a member of the demo crew named Dmitri."

Jamie closed the cottage door behind us. "Slow down . . . Who is missing?"

"They're not missing," I clarified. "They're just not here."

"And you think they're dead."

"No! I don't think they're dead. But Jason didn't show up for work this morning and he's dead, so I think you need to check on the others."

Jamie pulled out his notebook and pen again. "Okay, so a Dmitri."

"He was with the demo crew yesterday. Alex, the kid who helped you with the names, told me he wasn't at the place where they're staying this morning."

"All right. I'm sure Lieutenant Binder and Sergeant Flynn will follow up with him. Who was the next one?"

"Pru Caraway."

"Jason's wife?"

"Ex-wife. The mother of his kids, Ione and Kirk. They're young teenagers. I assume they're next of kin."

"Ms. Caraway was supposed to be here this morning?"

"She works in the kitchen with Livvie and Kathy. We waited for her at the town pier. She never showed up."

"Did you call her?"

"Livvie did. No answer." He wrote that down. "The next one is Terry Durand, Chris's brother."

"He was to work here today as well," Jamie confirmed.

"Yes and no."

Jamie was impatient. "What does that mean?"

"I was supposed to fire Terry this morning. I went by the *Dark Lady* where he's been living but he wasn't there." The boat wasn't there either, but I'd leave that detail for my interview with the state police. "So I went along to the town pier to stop him when he showed up for his ride out to the island, but he never showed."

"Wait, this is Chris's brother who just got out of prison? You were going to fire your boyfriend's brother?" Jamie was struggling to understand. "For what?"

I looked down at the line of flagstones that formed the path away from the cottage. I knew I'd have to tell this part, but I hadn't figured I'd be telling it so soon. "For fighting with Jason Caraway," I said. "That's why Terry was being fired."

I was the first one called up to the pavilion to be interviewed, as I expected since I'd found the body. Lieutenant Binder and Sergeant Flynn sat across a weathered picnic table from me. Flynn had a spiral pad in front of him and held a black ballpoint pen in his left hand.

We'd become friends over the last couple of years, but there was no small talk beyond a greeting. Binder led me step-by-step through the events of the morning. He was in his midforties, had a distinctive ski-slope nose, and a light brown fringe around his bald head. As I also expected, he stopped me when I got to the part about Terry not being at the marina when I went to fire him.

"Officer Dawes informs us that Mr. Durand was recently released from prison," Flynn said. He was younger than Lieutenant Binder, just a few years older than me. His brown hair was short and stood up straight, just like he did, as if it might be required to say the Pledge of Allegiance at any moment. His body testified to a highly disciplined diet and hours in the gym.

"That's correct," I answered.

"We'll look it up as soon as we get back to the mainland," Binder said, "but you might as well tell us, was he imprisoned for a violent crime?"

"He held up Hudson's, a gas station and mini-mart on the highway. A clerk was shot."

Flynn nodded. "We've been by that place loads of times. The clerk wasn't killed I assume, or Durand would still be inside."

"Injured," I confirmed. "Terry was released in late August."

"And you hired him?" Binder's mouth was set in a grim line under that distinctive nose.

"He's my boyfriend's brother. Besides, he's done his time."

Binder grunted. Neither he nor Flynn had thought much of Chris when they'd met. In fact, they'd nearly arrested him for a crime he hadn't committed. But over the time since then, a grudging respect had grown on each side.

"You say you planned to fire Mr. Durand because he fought with the victim." Flynn took us back to my description of events.

"Yes."

"Physically?" Flynn clarified.

"Yes."

"What was the fight about?" he pressed.

"You'd have to ask Terry." I had my own beliefs, but I didn't want to share my guesses with the police. Let Terry explain himself.

"We will." Flynn wrote it down.

Then Binder walked me through the rest of the morning from finding the body pretty much right up to the present moment. Flynn continued taking notes.

"Officer Dawes tells us you believe a member of the demolition team is absent today," Binder said.

I cleared my throat. "I met him yesterday. He translated for his boss."

"Can you describe him?"

"Midthirties, brown hair, tan-skinned, broad-shouldered, but not as big as some of the guys on the crew. About five ten. He spoke English without a Russian accent."

"Why did you speak with him?" Binder asked.

Another can of worms. "A hidden room was uncovered during the demolition at Windsholme. Mark Cochran, the general contractor; Wyatt Jayne, the architect; and I asked about it. The missing man, who I think is called Dmitri, spoke to us. His boss was with him, but Dmitri did most of the talking."

Binder and Flynn had been inside Windsholme before and after the fire and knew it well.

"A hidden room?" Binder said. "That place is like a labyrinth. What made it remarkable?"

"It wasn't just hidden. It was sealed off, closed up. And unlike every other room in the mansion, it wasn't empty. The original furnishings were there, the bedding, as well as personal belongings, presumably of a woman who stayed there in the late eighteen-nineties."

They looked at one another. "It's weird," I said. "But I don't think it has anything to do with this."

Binder gave me a look I had long ago learned to interpret as "we'll see," and went on with the interview.

When they were done they thanked me. "We'll talk again," Binder said.

"I have no doubt." I stood up and climbed back over the picnic bench. "Is there any chance it was a terrible accident?" It was strange, given the liability potentially involved, that this was, in my view, the best possible scenario.

Binder shut my hopes down quickly. "Highly unlikely. The ME currently believes Mr. Caraway suffered a fatal blow to the head and was dead before his body was moved and placed under the woodpile. He couldn't have hidden his own dead body."

Chapter Seven

It was late afternoon by the time Sonny, Livvie, Kathy, and I pulled up to the town pier in the Whaler. Jason's body had been removed from the island and the medical examiner had gone with it. The demo team was still being interviewed when Jamie told the rest of us we could go home. The Russians' interviews would be quick, with Alex translating. More in-depth questioning would have to wait until they were back on the mainland and an official state translator could be found.

Chris was waiting and swept me into his arms the minute I stepped onto the concrete pier. I'd called him as soon as I had cell service on the way home and asked him to meet me.

"What's going on?" He looked from one face to the other.

"Not here," I said. The poor communication from the island, along with the fact that the police activity was taking place out there, away from town eyes, had kept the news about Jason Caraway's murder quiet. That wouldn't last for long.

Livvie said she and Sonny would walk straight to Mom's house. "I just want to hug my kids," she said.

Chris and I sat in the cab of his pickup truck as the sun crept lower in the afternoon sky while I told him, in fits and starts, what had happened. I started with my trip to the marina that morning to fire Terry.

"Did you know Terry was taking the *Dark Lady* out sailing?" I asked.

"No," Chris admitted. "Not specifically. But he learned to sail on that boat like I did. He knows what he's doing." I could tell by the lines pinched together over his forehead that he was impatient. "You didn't call me to meet you at the pier because my brother went for a boat ride."

"I'll get there."

When I told him about discovering Jason's body, Chris drew back against the door of the truck, physically recoiling. The implications ticked across his face. "They'll look at Terry for this. Did you tell the cops about the fight yesterday?"

"I had to. There were over two hundred witnesses." I put a hand on his arm. "Binder and Flynn are still on the island. When they get back, they have to do the death notification. I imagine soon after that they'll start interviewing people in town."

He covered my hand with his own and gave it a squeeze. "I am so sorry I got you into this when I asked you to hire Terry."

"You didn't get me into this. Whoever killed Jason did. Let's not forget that. And Terry wasn't the only one who didn't show up for work this morning. Pru didn't, and one of the demo guys didn't."

"You don't think Pru—"

"No. I don't. My point is that being absent this morning doesn't make Terry guilty."

Chris was horrified. "I don't think he's guilty. Don't ever say that." He started the truck, shifted into drive, and pulled out of the parking space.

"Where are we going?"

"To the marina, of course, to tell Terry what's happened."

I opened my mouth and then shut it. Though Binder had asked me not to describe the body or its location on the island to other people or, especially, the press, he hadn't told me not to talk to Terry. What would I have done if the situation were reversed, if Livvie was a possible suspect in a murder? Gone to her immediately, no question.

As we drove to the marina, Mom called. "Livvie and Sonny told me what's happened. I am so sorry you had to go through that. And poor Pru and their kids."

And poor Emmy. She and Jason had been "seeing each other outside work." I'd dutifully given Binder and Flynn her contact information when they'd asked if I knew anything about Jason's social life. Should I call and give her a heads-up?

Mom continued talking. "Fee and Vee invited us all for dinner tonight. Before this happened, I said yes. Livvie and her family are going to go. She said it would be better than cooking. She's bushed."

I turned in my seat toward Chris. "Fee and Vee's for dinner tonight?"

He chuckled. "They want to hear about the murder."

"They invited us before they knew. What they really want is another installment from Lilly Smythe's journal."

He shrugged. "Your call. We've got to eat."

I was hopped up on caffeine and adrenaline. I hadn't

eaten anything except a bowl of blueberry grunt all day.
"We'll be there," I told Mom.

I was relieved to spot the *Dark Lady*'s mast as we
pulled into the marina parking lot. Thank goodness she
was back. I hoped that meant Terry was there, too.

From the dock, Chris called down to the cabin for
permission to come aboard, even though it was his boat.

Terry shouted, "Coming!" and we heard him climb
the cabin stairs. He smiled when he saw Chris. His face
fell when he spotted me. "Julia." His tone was curt.

"Terry."

"Can we go below?" Chris asked. "Julia has something to tell you."

Without a word, Terry turned and trudged down to
the cabin. "If you've come to tell me I'm fired, I already
figured that out."

"It's not that."

We stood in the cramped space. Chris and Terry faced
each other. They had different fathers and their faces
were completely different. Chris's shaggy brown hair
framed a face with features that were impossibly sym-
metrical. And there was that chin dimple. He was tan
from working outside for his landscaping business.
Terry's face was longer than Chris's, his features larger.
His blond hair was gray at the temples, which, along
with his lingering prison pallor, gave him a washed-out
look. His irises were green, but flecked and rimmed with
brown, not the intense emerald of Chris's and Vanessa's.

They did have almost identical physiques. They were
the same height, six-foot-two, and had the same rangy

bodies. Chris had earned his muscles at work. I suspected
Terry had spent a lot of his prison time working out.

"Jason Caraway is dead," I said.

"What? What happened?"

To my eye, Terry was genuinely shocked. I was in-
stantly sorry we had told him. I would've liked Binder
and Flynn to have seen his reaction. "He was murdered
on Morrow Island." I wasn't going any further, keeping
in mind the state police request not to.

Terry stood still. Time stood still. "What do you
mean?" he finally asked, voice shaking.

"Jason was murdered on Morrow Island," I repeated.

"When?"

Good question. "Sometime between when we all left
yesterday and when I found his body this morning."

"You found him?"

"Yes."

"Anybody arrested?"

"No."

"You're sure it was murder?"

"The detectives sounded, like, ninety-percent sure."

Terry pivoted and strode into the sleeping quarters.
He grabbed a duffel off one of the bunks and frantically
stuffed clothes and other belongings into it.

"What are you doing?" Chris demanded.

"Getting out of here."

Chris put a hand up to stop him as Terry charged back
into the main part of the cabin. "Don't."

"Get out of my way." Terry was under control, but
barely. He simmered with the same anger he'd directed
at Jason Caraway.

Chris dropped his hand but stood firmly in Terry's
path. "If you run you'll look guilty."

"If I stay, I'll be arrested."

"You didn't do it." Chris sounded like he had no doubt.

"That didn't help last time." Terry had gone to prison steadfastly maintaining his innocence.

"Let's be practical for a moment." Chris's voice was matter-of-fact, bringing the tension down in the little space. "You don't have a vehicle or more money than the few dollars in your pocket. Where will you get to that they won't find you?"

"It's easier to move in the shadows," Terry said.

"It's easier to move when you're not being hunted," Chris countered. "Listen a moment." He inclined his head toward me. "We know these cops. Flynn comes off like a hard-nose, but they're good guys. Julia has helped them in the past. She's good at solving stuff. They trust her. She'll help you. Julia will figure out who killed Jason."

My mouth hung open. While it was true I'd helped Binder and Flynn in the past, there was no guarantee I could figure out who the murderer was, or keep Terry from being arrested. "Chris—"

"You'll help him, right, Julia?"

Terry collapsed onto one of the stools next to the little eating table in the cabin. The fight seemed to have gone out of him. I looked from Chris to Terry and back again. "Okay," I said. "I'm in."

"Good," Chris said. "Where do we start?"

I sat on the stool across from Terry. "We start with Terry telling me the truth."

"Of course," Chris said for him. Terry was silent.

I forged ahead. "Why didn't you come to work this morning?"

Terry studied the tabletop. "I knew I was fired. I figured I'd save you the embarrassment."

"You were fired. But when I came to the marina this morning to tell you, the *Dark Lady* was gone. Where were you?"

"Sailing." Terry looked at Chris. "I'll pay you back for the fuel."

"Not if you run, you won't." Chris drilled his point home.

"Sailing," I said. "Where were you sailing? The police are going to want to know. And I need to know, too. We may be able to find people who saw you."

"Around the harbor," he answered. "I didn't go far. I wanted to clear my head is all."

"You never left the harbor?"

"Nope. Just tooled around. I knew Chris wouldn't want me taking her far."

That was good. If he stayed inside the big bowl of the outer harbor, it increased the chances others saw him, both from land and from other boats. And, if he hadn't sailed out of the mouth of the harbor, he couldn't have gotten to Morrow Island, so he couldn't have left Jason's body where I'd found it. No one could say they had seen him in the area.

"What started the fight with Jason yesterday?" I asked.

Terry didn't answer right away. Finally, he stroked his chin. "We just rubbed each other the wrong way."

"It was more than that. Was it about Emmy?"

"I don't like the way he treats her. Treated her," Terry corrected. "I could tell he was leading her on. What is a guy like that doing with a girl like her? He's fifteen years older than she is." Terry looked from my face to Chris's face and back again. He was Jason's age. He'd been fifteen years older than Emmy when Vanessa was conceived, if that's what had happened. "That's what I mean," he said, reading our looks correctly. "I was a bad guy then, and he's a bad guy now. Was a bad guy." He caught himself referring to Jason in the present tense again.

"But what started the fight, specifically?" I asked.

"Every night he breezes off and leaves her standing there. Last night, he's planning to leave with Sonny. Emmy's struggling with the stroller, diaper bag, the baby. So I went to help. Jason took exception. He came up behind me, pulled me around, and punched me."

"That's it? That's all you did to provoke him, help Emmy with her stuff?" Terry had done that after every clambake for a month.

Terry stared at the tabletop. "I may have mumbled something as I walked by him. Something like, 'You useless sack of—'"

We were all quiet for a moment. "And that was the only problem between you and Jason, the tension around the way he treated Emmy, and you insulting him last night?"

Terry picked up his head and looked me in the eyes. "I swear."

Chapter Eight

"Why did you tell your brother I could help him?" Chris and I were back in our apartment getting ready for dinner at the Snuggs'. We'd ridden home from the marina in silence.

Chris came out of the bathroom, a towel around his waist. "Because you can. You will."

"How did you know I'd do it? I certainly can't *guarantee* it."

"I knew you would do it because you love me. If the situation were reversed, I'd do anything for Livvie." He pulled a clean shirt and jeans out of the alcove where we stored our clothes in the studio apartment. "Are you going to change?"

"In a minute. You've known Livvie since she was in middle school. These last eighteen months you've seen her almost every day and spent every holiday with her. You hadn't laid eyes on your brother for ten years. I met him five weeks ago."

Chris had put on the jeans and was buttoning the flannel shirt. "None of that matters. I would help Livvie because she's your sister." He sounded hurt. Like, why were we even debating this?

A wave of tiredness hit me. I dropped onto our old, beat-up couch. The springs were gone and I landed with a thud. "Chris, we don't know he's innocent. He and your boat were gone this morning."

Chris was defiant. "He explained that." But then his expression softened. He sat down next to me and pulled on his socks and boots. "Look, Julia, I'm not naive. Terry has a troubled history. He may dispute what happened at Hudson's ten years ago, but the store clerk identified him. I take his claims of innocence with a grain of salt. But I don't see him murdering Jason. Terry's not like that."

"He's been in prison for a decade, and you were sporadically in touch with him for years before that. I'm not sure you can say what he's like."

We lapsed into silence, both of us exhausted. "I'll do what I can," I said quietly. "But if he did it, I'm not going to help him get away with it."

Chris sat back, shocked. "I'm not asking you to do that. I never would."

"Okay then. I'll get started in the morning."

We gathered at Mom's house and crossed the street to the Snuggles Inn together. Mom and Tallulah walked with Marguerite. Livvie herded a reluctant Page while Sonny carried Jack. Sonny and Livvie both looked done in. Chris and I brought up the rear. I must have looked as tired as they did.

Vee threw open their front door. "How delightful to see you!"

Her sister Fee stood in their large entrance hall, taking drink orders. The sisters were a study in contrasts. Vee was always glamorous, dressed to the nines, her snow-white hair swept up in a chignon. Fee preferred the company of their succession of Scottish terriers, the current one named Mackie, to people. Plain-faced and outdoorsy, she strode around the harbor hills with Mackie, despite the arthritis in her spine that bent her over.

The house smelled of tomato and garlic, an amazing dinner to come. Vee wasn't going to be outdone by Chris.

Like us, the Snuggs were in transition from their tourist season to their off-season lives. In the summer they shared the windowed study at the back of the first floor as a bedroom so all the rooms upstairs could be rented. They were still sleeping in the back room, because the inn was full on the weekends with leaf peepers and folks trying to grab onto the last of the beautiful days. But on a Monday night, the B and B was empty of guests, the way I preferred it. Much as I loved visiting in the summer when Vee made her wonderful English breakfasts, it was lovely to have the old Victorian house feeling like a home again, even if it was only until the weekend.

The sisters ushered us into their living room. The Snuggs still used the antique furniture their parents had brought over when the family had moved from England so Fee and Vee's father could work as the golf pro at Busman's Harbor Country Club. Sonny put Jack on the Oriental rug. He couldn't yet crawl, but he had perfected a rolling-over motion that got him around quite efficiently. He immediately approached Mackie, who unlike some terriers, was a patient and tolerant dog, used to

B and B guests including little kids. Lots of B and Bs in the harbor didn't accept children, but the Snuggs said the kind of parents who would bring their family to stay at a place without a pool or TVs in the rooms inevitably had lovely children.

We gathered around the big oval table in the dining room, which was as old-fashioned and homey as the rest of the inn. Dinner turned out to be halibut pizzaiola, which Vee served with orzo and broccoli. The halibut filets were perfect, bought fresh that day from Ferguson's Fish Market, I was certain. They stood up beautifully to the tomato-y flavor of the pizzaiola sauce.

"Delicious," Marguerite said. "I've eaten seafood all my life and I've never had this dish before, but I hope to have it again."

In the short time that Livvie, Sonny, and I had been back in town, word had spread about Jason Caraway's murder. Questioned by Vee, each of us told some of the story. Sonny's sadness at the loss of his friend cast a gloom over the room.

By the time we finished telling what we could, the main course was finished. "Let's talk of happier things," Marguerite said. "Or at least less recent things. Would you like to hear more of the journal?"

The Snugg sisters feigned delight, as if it wasn't the main reason we'd been invited. Chris and Tallulah cleared the table, letting Sonny, Livvie, and I sit, for which I was extremely grateful. Vee served coffee and dessert, a plate of dried fruits and cheeses.

Marguerite brought the journal out of the bag Tallulah had carried across the street. "Shall we start?" Her eyes were bright behind her reading glasses.

"June 23, 1898

"The house is as grand from the inside as it is from the outside, though the atmosphere is informal. There are often maids to be found on the front staircase, or yacht crewmen hanging about in the kitchen. I doubt life is like that in the house in Back Bay. Mrs. Stout is a good woman. Everything she cooks is tasty whether for the family or the servants.

"I have experienced both, for as usual, I exist between worlds, no one quite knowing what to do with me. I sleep on the family floor, but in a small room off the nursery. The nursery is unused now, except for my lessons with William and Charles when we are forced by the weather to stay indoors. The young men have their own bedrooms. There was a little sister who died of scarlet fever. Despite its size the old nursery has a gloomy feel and I take the young men outdoors for their lessons as often as I can.

"The death of her daughter must explain the sadness I sense around the younger Mrs. Morrow. She is retiring and spends much of her day in a rocker on the front porch, lost in a novel. The boys, William and Charles, are both bright and willing students. William is a bit of a bully toward his younger brother, who is sweet-natured and sensitive. Mr. Morrow has expressed the hope that William will serve as Charles's protector when they are away at school, but I believe Charles will be relieved to have a cohort of his own friends around him to dilute William's looming presence.

"*Mrs. Morrow the older acts as if she still runs the house and no one puts her in check. The younger Mrs. Morrow is too detached, whether that is the cause or the effect. Mr. Morrow is either too busy or does not want to disturb the detente that has settled in the household. Young Mr. Frederick seems to enjoy the current setup, with his doting mother ruling the roost.*

"*He is often out sailing in the small sailboat or playing croquet on the lawn with the young men, or swimming off the little beach on the other side of the island. He makes a dashing figure.*

"*The staff is pleasant enough, although the housekeeper, Mrs. Franklin, is feckless and absentminded, not good qualities in someone who must manage the household. I doubt she will last the summer. The maids are pleasant, cheery girls who love flirting with the crewmen, who flirt back. The yacht captain is a bit like myself, neither one thing nor the other. He is a Navy man and well educated. Like me, an employee, but not a servant. He has an impressive brown beard and intelligent blue eyes that laugh when he does. Though we are both consigned to limbo, we have not become friends as we see each other infrequently.*

"*I write this in my little room off the nursery. It is quite pleasant, especially in the morning when the window lets in bright sunlight, which I think must be why it is placed so strangely. It is too high in the wall for me to see out, though I can always go into the nursery if I need to. I have to open and close it with a tall stick that resides*

*in the room for this purpose. There is a door in
the wall that connects my little room to the
bedroom next door. It is locked but sometimes I
hear Mr. Frederick moving around in there,
which is disconcerting."*

"There was no door to the room next door," Tallulah
protested.

"It must have been sealed up, too," Mom said.

"So strange." Livvie's brow was creased, wondering
about it as we all were.

Marguerite put the journal down. "I think that's
enough for now. I believe we've leaned on your hospi-
tality long enough."

Fee and Vee rushed to assure her that we hadn't, but
Marguerite was plainly tired, so they gave in easily. Jack
was asleep on Livvie's lap and Page on the living room
couch. We said our good-byes and Tallulah and Mom
escorted Marguerite across the street.

I stood with Livvie as she put Jack into his car seat.
"What do you make of this fascination with the journal?"
she asked.

"It's harmless," I said. "It keeps everyone busy and
their minds off the murder."

"I hope so," she answered, and climbed behind the
steering wheel.

Chapter Nine

The next morning Chris went off to work, but I grabbed a stool at the counter at Gus's restaurant downstairs from my apartment. Gus, my irascible landlord, was behind the counter working the grill top as he did seven days a week, 6:00 a.m. to 3:00 p.m., every month of the year except February, when he and Mrs. Gus took off to visit the families of their middle-aged kids who lived in warmer places.

Though the restaurant was crowded, Gus poured me a cup of coffee and handed me a pitcher of cream without me asking for it. "On your own?" he asked, glancing toward the door at the bottom of the stairs to my apartment.

"Yes. I've got some thinking to do."

"I imagine you do. I hear Jason Caraway's body was found on Morrow Island. Murder, they say."

"So it's all over town."

He waved the coffeepot, taking in all the people at the counter and in the dining room beyond it. "It's everywhere. Biggest conversational item by far when I went around to take orders. The news has to be big to get Mainers off the topic of the weather."

I smiled. What he said was true.

"I hear Jason had a fight with your boyfriend's brother the day before he was killed." I didn't deny it, so Gus went on. "Seems like that makes him the obvious suspect, what with his record and all."

"There are other suspects." My tone was a little too defensive. I looked around to make sure no one was listening. The people on the stools on either side of me were in deep conversations with their neighbors. "I'm not sure the police have even interviewed Terry yet. If he was so obvious, they would have had him into the station last night."

Gus shrugged. "If you say so. What're you havin'?"

Gus's menu hadn't changed since I learned to read. It probably hadn't changed for fifty years. The prices had crept up, but not much. He only took cash. No credit cards, no checks, and definitely no fancy cash apps.

"I need to think. So, protein."

"Eggs then. How?"

"Over-easy. Wheat toast."

"Home fries?"

"No, I want to travel light."

Once he'd gone, I started thinking about how I could help Terry. I'd assured Gus there were other suspects. Who were they? The obvious ones were the other two people who hadn't shown up for work the day the body was found: Pru Caraway and Dmitri no-last-name-yet from the demo crew. Of the two, Pru was far more obvious. She was the victim's ex-wife and involved in the quadrangle of tension: Jason—Emmy—Terry—Pru. The demo guy was a long shot. What possible motive could he have? But the look that had passed between

him and Jason at the fire was seared in my memory. I
would have to find out something about Dmitri's background and current circumstances.

Gus put the eggs down in front of me, cooked to per-
fection as always. I picked up my fork, pierced the
yolks, and watched them run onto the plate. The sunny
yellow color of the eggs made me feel more optimistic
before I even took a bite. Gus returned to refill my coffee.
I dug in.

If I considered Pru as a suspect, did I have to consider
Emmy? She was the mother of my niece's best friend,
and possibly, the mother of my boyfriend's niece as
well. I didn't want to think too hard about it. She had
characterized her relationship with Jason in casual
terms, "seeing each other outside work." What did that
mean, exactly? Would that level of relationship provide
enough motive to kill? Of course, she could have lied.
Even if I didn't consider her a viable suspect, I had to
talk to her. She could give me background about what
was going on with Jason, his state of mind, current activities, and so on.

As could my brother-in-law, Sonny, who'd worked
with Jason at the clambake fire for years.

These were not brilliant insights, but it was enough
to get started. I would leave calling on Pru for last. Hers
was a house of mourning. She and her kids had only
heard the news about Jason's murder last night. Friends
and family would be gathered, even possibly Livvie,
who had worked with Pru in the clambake kitchen for
two seasons. It would be intrusive to visit this morning,
especially to ask questions that might be considered in-
sensitive.

I had no idea where to find the Russians when they

weren't at work. Maybe Mark or Wyatt would know. Sonny was probably out in his father's lobster boat. Emmy was probably at home with her kids.

I paid my bill and walked to Mom's house. Everything was quiet and her car wasn't in its place in the old triple-bay garage out back. It was a gorgeous fall day. She must have taken Marguerite and Tallulah on an outing, maybe to visit the beautiful lighthouse at Pemaquid Point and then to lunch in Damariscotta afterward—Mom's usual outing with guests from out of town.

I climbed the back stairs at Mom's to the Snowden Family Clambake office on the second floor. My dad had been dead six years, but neither Mom nor I had changed a thing in the office since he'd worked there. I liked to feel his comforting presence as I went about managing the business. I often asked his advice. He never answered directly, but saying the words aloud, forming them into a question he would understand, usually helped me find the answer.

There wasn't much to do at this time of year. The next bake wasn't until Saturday, and there were only the three over the Columbus Day weekend for the rest of the season. In the off-season, Chris and I ran a dinner restaurant in Gus's space. It was meant to provide locals with a gathering place after the more touristy restaurants shut down. We'd spent a lot of time in late September planning for the new season and ordering nonperishables. Now there was little to do until we opened.

I called the director of excursions at the cruise ship headquarters in Jacksonville. I was worried about what to say. Hasty assurances that the situation the day before would never happen again, I supposed. That had to be true.

"Julia! I heard about the murder."

I had hoped the passengers were back safely aboard the ship before news had spread around the harbor about the murder on Morrow Island.

"You've heard," I confirmed.

"A couple of our crew spotted the police activity on your island. I couldn't reach you so I called the Tourist Bureau, who told me."

Great. I hadn't noticed the missed calls from her when I'd returned to the mainland the day before. "You understand then, why we had to cancel at the last minute."

"Of course, of course."

"Because we love having you. We hope you'll book again next year."

"We'll see," she chirped.

I doubted we'd ever hear from her again.

Le Roi, the Maine coon cat, padded into the office and jumped into my lap. He had a knack for knowing when I needed cheering up. He was almost thirty pounds of long-haired cat, so there wasn't really room for him on my lap, but I let him stay. I'd missed him. Le Roi, named for Elvis, the King, was indeed the King of Morrow Island. In the summer he had the run of the place and his pick of easy marks to cage bits of clam and lobster from. He'd spent his first six winters with the island caretakers, but a year ago that had become impossible, so Le Roi had spent last winter with me.

I loved the arrangement and so did Le Roi. The only problem was Le Roi didn't love Chris. Or like him. Le Roi loathed Chris. The big cat's attitude was that he and I were a duo. Chris was the interloper. Le Roi had staked his claim by lying crosswise on Chris's side of the bed and going limp as a demonstrator practicing peaceful resistance when Chris tried to move him. He hid Chris's keys, money, and wallet. Finally the situation had escalated to the point that Chris couldn't put his boots on in the morning without checking inside them first.

So Le Roi was spending this off-season at Mom's, where he got exclusive time with me when I worked.

I gave him a pat and called Mark Cochran. If anyone knew where the demo crew was lodged it was him. His young, male receptionist informed me Mark was at a job site off the peninsula all day. He'd return all calls the next morning.

I didn't want to talk to the receptionist about the Russians—the fewer people I involved in these conversations, the better—so I thanked him and hung up. There was one other person who might know about the demo crew. I set Le Roi on the floor, went to get my new (to me) Subaru from my mother's garage where I kept it, and drove out to Westclaw Point.

Chapter Ten

I pulled into the sandy double track that served as a driveway for Quentin Tupper's house on the outer end of Westclaw Point. I was pleased to see Quentin's old wooden-sided station wagon in the drive. Wyatt used it when she was in town. She was probably in.

I climbed the steps of Quentin's marble and glass edifice and followed the decking around to the ocean side of the house. Through the glass front door I spotted Wyatt in the kitchen. I used a knuckle to rap on the pane.

She looked up sharply. This far from town, in a house facing the water, privacy was assumed. She wore a light-weight, belted bathrobe and sleek black slippers. She was unmade-up, but her hair was brushed and, as always, gorgeous.

"Julia! I'm surprised to see you here."

I couldn't say, "I was in the neighborhood." Nobody was this far out by happenstance, so I said, "I want to talk. Do you have a few minutes?"

Wyatt stepped back to let me in. Quentin's house never failed to impress, with its soaring ceilings and natural materials. Wyatt and Quentin were old friends.

This house had been her first architectural commission. Quentin was long gone for the season, sailing his boat the *Flittermouse* to warmer places. Wyatt used the house when she was in town.

Wyatt and I had history, too. We'd been assigned as roommates our freshman year in boarding school. It hadn't gone well, and by midyear I'd moved out, given a single by a sympathetic housing officer. I'd been flabbergasted when Quentin had recommended Wyatt as the architect for Windsholme. I hadn't known they knew each other. But in round two on our journey, Wyatt and I were doing much better. We were both older and wiser.

"I hear work is at a standstill on Windsholme," she said. Not, "It's horrible that poor man is dead," or even, "I heard you found the body. How awful."

It was the kind of thing that would have set me off years earlier, causing me to ruminate about how egotistical she was, how it was always about her and her interests. Now that I understood her better I knew she wasn't self-centered so much as laser focused. Her focus and drive made me comfortable trusting her with our enormous, complicated renovation, not to mention the huge sum of money it required.

"You've heard," I confirmed. "There was a murdered man found on the island. No one's allowed to go out there until the cops are done."

"Which will be when?"

"I'll check in with them this afternoon and see if I can get you a date."

She led me to the massive kitchen island and offered me coffee from Quentin's fancy machine. I said no, thank you, I'd had plenty at Gus's that morning. "You don't mind if I help myself," she said.

"Of course not."

We settled onto the high stools at the island. She turned to face me. "I've been thinking about the secret room," she said. "We'll need to get all of that stuff out of there to continue the demo. As soon as we can get back on the island, we should photograph everything in the room, exactly as we found it. Then we should bring it all back to the mainland."

"I guess." She was right. The room had to be emptied, but it seemed so precipitous to remove stuff that had sat there undisturbed for over a century within a few days of stumbling across it.

Wyatt didn't catch my hesitation. "Where do you want to store it?"

"Mom's until we sort it and take whatever we're going to keep," I answered after a moment's consideration. I wasn't certain how Mom would feel about that, but she was the only one who had space. "Then we'll let the historical society take whatever they want." I paused. "That's not actually why I'm here."

Wyatt wrinkled her pert nose. "If not Windsholme, then what?"

"What do you know about the team doing the demolition?"

Her perfectly shaped brows flew up her forehead. "You don't think they had anything to do with the body!"

"That's for the police to worry about," I said, which was true. "But aside from that, what do you know about them?"

"They're Russian, but you know that." She scrunched her brow, thinking. "They strictly do demo, no other part of the job. They move from town to town, season to season. We attracted them here with the work on Windsholme and Rosehill Cottage." The other renovation

Wyatt was working on locally. "Mark Cochran uses them a lot. You should talk to him."

"I will. He's at a job site all day and he isn't taking calls," I answered. "Do you know where the crew is staying locally?"

"Why?" She was immediately suspicious.

"I want to talk to them about what they saw the morning of . . . you know."

"You're butting in to the murder investigation," she accused.

"Don't be so judgmental. You were once the beneficiary of me butting in," I reminded her.

She grunted. "As you say." Even her grunts were somehow feminine.

"Mark owns a house on Bayview Street, the white one in the middle of the second block from the water. He's flipping it eventually, but right now he's using it to house his crews as they come through. The Russians can walk from there to the marina to take the beat-up boat Mark found for them out to your island. They live together, commute together, work together."

"Must be intense."

She gave me a quizzical look. "Don't you live with Chris and run a restaurant with him?"

"Only in the off-season. We don't commute together." Unless you counted walking down the stairs from our apartment.

"That's right, I forgot." Wyatt's tone was as dry as the Sahara. "During the season you work with and commute with the rest of your family."

Bayview Street was in town, an easy walk from my mother's, so I took my car back to her garage. My plan was to go straight to visit the demo team, but as I walked down Mom's driveway toward the street, Sonny pulled up in his pickup.

"Hey, Julia." He climbed out of the cab.

"Hey, Sonny."

"Hauled some traps for Dad this morning. Thought I'd come over to your mother's and take the screens off the front porch, since we can't run the clambake."

"That'll make Mom happy." Taking down the screens and stowing the porch furniture was a fall ritual.

We stood for a moment in silence. Sonny looked terrible. His shoulders were hunched and he stared at the ground. Even his normally fiery red hair looked dull.

"I'm sorry about your friend," I said.

"I'll miss him, Julia. I'll miss his skill at the clambake fire, and I'll miss his company." He stuttered out the last bit, voice heavy with emotion.

"How long have you known Jason?"

"He started at the clambake ten years ago, if you can believe it. Your dad was the bakemaster then. Jason and I were both learning. He took to it easily. More easily than I did. He stayed on after your dad died and I was grateful to him."

"I often wondered why he stayed," I said. "For sure he would have made more money if he'd used those same hours for lobstering."

Sonny nodded. "Me too. Especially these last couple of years when he's had that big new boat. He's obviously doing great with his traps. To tell the truth, I never wanted to ask him why he stayed. I was afraid if I brought up the subject, it would get him wondering. I didn't want that. I needed his help. For sure I thought he might leave when he and Pru divorced. Morrow Island is small and it was a rough time, from what he told me."

"What happened with them?"

Sonny shrugged. "You know. They married young. Outgrew each other. It happens—" He spotted my scowl. He and Livvie had married young. Too young, my parents thought. "Happens to *some* people," he hastily amended.

"Were there other women?"

Sonny shook his head. "You know Jason. He'd flirt with anything that moved. I heard rumors, but he never said anything to me directly."

"Do you have any idea who could have killed him?"

Sonny stepped back, crossing his big arms across his chest. "I have a very good idea. So do you."

"You think Terry killed him."

"I guess you're gonna defend the guy because he's Chris's brother. You saw the same fight I did, felt the same tension. Terry just got out of prison for Pete's sake. Wake up and smell the homicide, Julia."

I'd figured he would feel that way. Sonny hadn't liked Terry from the start, which was mostly my fault because I'd forced Terry on him. "Let's not jump to conclusions," I cautioned. "You don't know he did it."

Sonny shoved his hands in the pockets of his down vest. "You don't know he didn't."

I admitted that was true. "Sonny, I'm not trying to ruin your friend's reputation after he's gone, or blame the victim for his own murder. I simply want an understanding of who Jason was. A complete one."

The air went out of him then, and he relented. "Jason's ten years older than me. More than that, twelve years. I didn't know him growing up. I heard he was wild as a teenager, always in trouble. And maybe that continued on after he was an adult, for a while. Maybe. But I never saw a bit of it. He was honest in his dealings with me, gave me a full day's work for a full day's pay, just like he did for your dad. I never had reason to complain."

"What does 'wild' mean?" I asked. "And how recently is 'continued on after'? Up to now?"

Sonny sighed. A sad sigh. He was so full of bluster normally. "Why don't you ask your cop friends?" he said.

"Binder and Flynn? What do they know?"

"Not them. The local cops. Ask your friend Jamie and Pete Howland what they know about Jason."

Chapter Eleven

If Mark Cochran was flipping the house the demo guys were staying in on Bayview Street, I could see why he'd gotten it cheaply. The dirty, white shingles were broken and half the green shutters on the front of the house hung off or were absent all together. The steps to the porch didn't look safe.

Fortunately, I didn't have to climb them. Four men were seated on the sagging front porch, while a fifth, a giant with bulging muscles, tended unidentifiable meat on a grill, presumably for lunch. There was a bottle of vodka on the porch floor next to the crew chief's chair. They'd started early.

As I approached, the boss made a simple gesture with his hand and Alex, the slender young guy who'd translated the day before, came down the steps.

"Hello," he said. "How are you today?"

"Oh, you know, doing about normal for the day after a murder." His sharp-featured face made it clear my attempt at humor didn't translate and I regretted it. "I'm fine."

"Good." He turned his head from side to side, scanning the street, wondering what had brought me there, no doubt.

"Did you find your friend, Dmitri, the one who was missing from the job yesterday?"

Alex shook his head. "No. He wasn't here when we got back and he hasn't turned up since."

"That's a little odd, isn't it? That he should disappear like that."

Alex glanced back at the crew chief. There was no question who the alpha was in the group, not just at work, but also in all things, including conversations on the lawn he wasn't even involved in.

Alex bent his head toward me. "No. I do not think it is unusual. We have been expecting it for a while."

An unexpected answer. "Why?"

Alex tilted his head back toward the men on the porch. "Joe and Yuri are brothers. Oleg is their brother-in-law. I am their cousin. We all come from the same village. You understand?"

I nodded to show that I did. "You're all connected. But not Dmitri."

"No. He showed up at a job site about six months ago looking for work. We had many big jobs, so Joe took him on. He wasn't one of us."

"At Windsholme yesterday, Joe brought him to speak to us about the sealed-off room," I said.

"That is because Dmitri's English is very good. He was born here. His parents are Russian so he speaks the language, but, as you can see, he was different. I thought he might leave as easily as he came, and then he did. He's gone off for a few days before, but he's always come back. Maybe he will this time, but I think not."

"Is his stuff gone?"

"Most of it. He never had much. A few clothes, his phone." Alex shrugged. Dmitri's was a life on the road, not weighed down by possessions.

"It seems odd he would have disappeared on the day of the murder," I said.

"He wouldn't have known that, would he, if he had left before it happened?"

He had a point.

Alex looked back again at the boss, who nodded, then turned back to me. "Would you like to stay for lunch? We enjoy the day. No work at your beautiful house and our other job here hasn't started."

"That's very kind, but I have to go. Have you talked to the police today?"

He shook his head. "No, not since our interviews yesterday."

I stared at the bottle next to the crew chief. "You might want to go easy on that vodka in case the cops show up with the translator for follow-ups."

Alex nodded. "I will tell this to Joe."

From Bayview Street, I walked the few blocks to the police station. Marge Brown, the civilian receptionist, was at her desk. I asked to see Lieutenant Binder or Sergeant Flynn.

Marge took a dim view of my relationship with Binder and Flynn, but today she was all sweetness and light. "You're in luck. They're both here. They haven't been most of the day. I'll let them know." She picked up the handset from the console on her desk. "Julia Snowden here to see you." She replaced it and said, "Go in."

I entered the big multipurpose room the Major Crime Unit used as an office when they were in town. They had their usual long tables set up side-by-side to use as desks, with a whiteboard across from it and the miserable folding chairs where they and their interviewees sat. In the corner opposite, at the far end of the room, there was something new. Two more tables set up in a V shape, with laptops on their surfaces and power cords snaking to an extension and surge protector below.

"Julia Snowden," Binder called. "What brings you to visit?"

I went over to them. "I'm wondering when we can get back to Morrow Island," I said. "The demo crew is idle and the general contractor and architect are worried about the schedule if the demo isn't done, the debris removed, and the house buttoned up before the weather turns."

"It's not clear yet when you can return," Binder answered. They both had their jackets off in the windowless room, and their shirtsleeves rolled up.

I sat down in the folding chair facing them. "So it was definitely murder."

"No doubt. Caraway was killed by a deliberate blow to the head by something heavy and metal."

"Sounds like the sledgehammers the demo crew uses," I said.

"Or like the hatchets Sonny and his team use around the clambake fire. Or any number of other tools you keep stored on your island." He paused. "They're all being tested. Sonny has the receipt. But I doubt we'll find anything. The real weapon is probably long gone."

I digested that. "Where was Jason killed?"

Binder hesitated. "Some ways from where he was found." When I didn't say anything he relented and gave me a little more. "Not far from the dock. That's as specific as I'm going to get."

"What time was he killed?" I asked.

Flynn looked at Binder and then answered. "Three hours before you found him. Four at the outside."

"So before the demo crew arrived." Flynn and I had made a lot of progress in a couple of years. Binder had always been supportive of my interest in their cases. Early on, getting Flynn to tell me anything had been like pulling teeth. Now he trusted me at least a little.

"*Say* they arrived," Flynn corrected. "Yes."

"That guy Dmitri is still missing," I told them.

Binder sat up straighter. That would have been a physical impossibility for Flynn.

"How do you know that?" Lieutenant Binder ran a hand over his scalp. "Have you talked with them since the day of the murder? Julia, why are you in the middle of this?"

I was about to say, "Because the murder was on my island," but Flynn beat me to the punch. "She thinks Chris's brother, Terry Durand, is a suspect."

"Is he?" I asked.

"Let's see." Flynn gazed at the high ceiling before looking back at me, his eyes drilling into mine. "Durand had a fistfight with the victim the day before the murder and he's been convicted of a violent crime. So yes, we need to consider that he might have done it."

"There are others," Binder added. I couldn't tell if it was the truth or if it was an attempt to reassure me. I did not feel reassured.

"What's going on over there?" I pointed to the tables and laptops in the opposite corner.

"Other cops," Flynn answered. "More cops."

"State cops?" I asked.

Binder stood. "That's all you're getting today. Thanks for coming in."

When I left the multipurpose room, Marge's desk was empty. I peered around the piece of cubicle wall that separated the civilian receptionist from the big, windowed bullpen the entire Busman's Harbor police force shared. Chief Beaupre had his own desk, set off in the corner, which he needed because his life was ruled by schedules, budgets, and reports. He hated tourists and scowled from Memorial Day to Columbus Day. He had less than a week to survive until he could smile again.

The rest of the department shared two metal desks that were piled with files, computer gear, and office supplies. There were only seven sworn officers during the fall, winter, and spring, and they spent most of their time out on patrol, on foot or by car. The office was for interviews and report-writing only. It was empty.

Sonny had said to ask Jamie and Pete Howland about Jason. I'd obviously come at the wrong time. I'd have to wait for shift change to find them. I was headed out of the station when I spotted a patrol car pulling into the parking lot. Pete Howland was at the wheel. He and Jamie got out of the car.

I walked toward them. Jamie stopped on the sidewalk to wait for me. "Hi, Julia. What's up?"

"I was looking for you two. Sonny told me to ask you and Howland about Jason Caraway. He hinted Jason had a reputation, or worse, when he was younger."

Jamie wrinkled his forehead. "I'd never heard anything. I don't know why Sonny told you to talk to me."

"You haven't heard anything?" Pete Howland came

and stood behind Jamie. "Then I haven't trained you very well."

I turned my attention to Pete. "You know about Jason's past?"

Howland looked toward the town-hall-firehouse-police-station building. "I'm happy to fill you in, but maybe can we go someplace not so public?"

"Pete—" Jamie cautioned.

"You're here because you're helping Terry Durand." Howland waited for me to acknowledge it. "Then there are some things you should know." Then he beelined down the sidewalk toward Main Street and kept going.

I hurried to catch up to him. Jamie followed right behind me. When we reached him, Howland said, "Let's keep walking."

We followed him like lost puppies along Main Street, until we got past the retail blocks and the activity died down. At that point Howland slowed his pace and began to talk. "Did you know I was the arresting officer when Terry Durand got picked up?"

I shook my head. "No, Pete, I didn't know that." I'd asked him about Jason, not Terry, but it seemed worth hearing him out.

"I'd been on the force less than a month, just out of the academy, when we got a call from neighbors about a shot fired at Hudson's. I was the first officer on the scene and I was shaking in my boots when I went in there. Terry was in the store. When he saw me he put his hands in the air. He stayed while I called for an ambulance and waited for backup. I didn't take the time to cuff him. The clerk was hurt bad and needed my attention."

Howland stopped and stood in the middle of the deserted sidewalk. "Of course, I did everything wrong."

He looked at Jamie, who nodded his confirmation. "I should have secured Durand first. What if he decided to shoot me? But he seemed as freaked out as I was. I honestly think the gun going off was an accident."

"He was convicted," I said.

"Yup," Howland agreed. "I testified at his trial. Armed robbery and aggravated assault with a firearm."

"He brought that gun into the market. He was responsible for whatever happened after, whether he meant to do it or not," Jamie said.

"I know all this," I said. "Not in the detail you do, but I know the broad outlines. What does it have to do with Jason?"

"This is what I'm telling you," Howland insisted. "Before Terry shot that guy . . . What was his name?" Howland resumed walking, though at a slower pace. Jamie and I followed.

"Gray," Jamie said. "Christopher Gray. He was only twenty years old." Jamie hadn't been on the force when Terry was arrested. He hadn't joined until years later. Which told me he'd looked at Terry's case file recently. Since Terry had come back to town. Or even since the murder.

"Anyway," Howland continued, "before that happened Terry and Jason were best friends."

"Wait." I stopped in my tracks. "Terry and Jason were buddies?" Terry had sworn to me that there was nothing between them except the Emmy thing. I was shocked, though I tried not to let Jamie and Howland know it.

"They did a bunch of stupid stuff together," Howland answered, "burgling summer residences, petty theft. The gun Terry used in the robbery was stolen from a summer house. No one ever got hurt. No one was even home when these burglaries happened. But we had our eyes on them. Chief Beaupre, in particular, was convinced the two of them were up to no good."

Howland started walking again, but it was my turn to stand still. Keeping my voice even, I asked, "Do the police believe Jason and Terry's friendship extended to the present?"

Howland frowned. "Julia, this is not an official police briefing. Why do you think we're not in the station? I know you're trying to help your boyfriend's brother. I'm a friend of Sonny's and I'd like to think I'm a friend of yours. I am trying to tell you, unofficially, what you might be getting yourself into."

"I appreciate it." I did. The three of us began to walk again. On the quiet end of Main Street, stately sea captain's homes stood on either side of the road. Nowadays, most were inns. A few had been converted to vacation condominiums with water views.

"The point of telling you this," Howland said, "is that after the clerk was shot, Jason Caraway cut off his relationship with Terry Durand, one hundred percent. He never visited him in county jail. He didn't attend one minute of Terry's trial. As far as I've heard, he never visited Terry in the state prison at Warren."

"That seems cold, if they were such buddies," Jamie said.

"We figured, or I should say people more experienced than me who knew them better, figured Jason was freaked out by the idea of armed robbery, much less someone ending up shot," Howland said. "It was way beyond anything the two of them had done before. Jason was married by then with two young kids. It made sense that he broke off with Terry."

"And the Busman's PD never suspected Jason of anything after that?" I thought about that big, fancy lobster boat, the *Money Honey*.

"If he was doing anything recently, he's much cleverer about it than when he was young. I've never heard a word against him in the station house." Howland turned to Jamie. "You?"

"Nothing," Jamie agreed.

By then we were almost to the point where Main Street met the highway out of town. "Thanks," I said.

"We've got to get back." Jamie was fidgety, anxious to return to the station. I was sure they both had work to do.

"You guys go ahead," I said. "I'm going to walk a little."

Chapter Twelve

After Jamie and Howland speed-walked away, I turned back toward town. I climbed up the harbor hill past Mom's house and down the other side past Gus's. I told myself I didn't know where I was going, but I did. Like a heat-seeking missile, I ended up at the marina. I was furious with Terry.

He had lied to me outright about his relationship with Jason. This is what came of trusting an ex-con, a man I barely knew.

I was relieved when I saw the *Dark Lady*, bobbing at her berth. I didn't politely ask permission to come aboard, just shouted, "Terry, I need to speak to you!"

He came quickly up the cabin stairs. He was dressed in jeans and a T-shirt, and held a dirty rag, like he'd been cleaning something. "Julia?"

"We need to talk, Terry." I stepped onto the boat. "I just came from the police station."

"Me too. They had me in late this morning for what they called a 'chat.' Asked me a million questions about my fight with Jason."

"You shouldn't talk to them without a lawyer present."

"I can't afford a lawyer. You should know that."

"Don't be stupid, Terry." I stepped closer to him. "You lied to me about your relationship with Jason."

His mouth opened in surprise. He took a step backward on the small deck. The steps to the cabin were directly behind him. I grabbed his arm to stop his movement. I had a vision of him tumbling down.

"Thanks."

When he didn't say anything else, I continued. "You and Jason were old friends. You were buddies until he married and had his kids and you—"

"Went to prison," Terry finished.

"Why didn't you tell me the truth?"

He stared at the deck. "Because it doesn't matter. It has nothing to do with this thing with Emmy. It definitely doesn't have anything to do with his murder."

"How can you say that? From what I heard, Jason abandoned you when you were arrested. You must have resented him. At least that's what the police are going to say."

Terry stared at a spot in the water off the starboard side and said nothing.

"When I volunteered to help"—I didn't bother to disguise my anger—"I asked you for one thing. I asked you to tell me the truth about you and Jason."

"You didn't volunteer." Terry was angry, too. "Chris volunteered you." He brought his eyes up to meet mine. "You don't want to do this anymore than I want you doing it."

That set me off. "Why wouldn't you want help?"

"Help!" he cried. "Do you even know what help is? You're supposed to be finding out things that make me look less guilty, not *more* guilty."

I brought my voice down, low and direct. "Did you

kill Jason Caraway? Is that why you don't want me poking around?" It was a terrible accusation to make toward anyone, much less someone you hoped you might someday be related to.

His voice, when he finally spoke, was deadly quiet. "I did not kill Jason Caraway. I took a minor dig at him that he overreacted to. Period. End of story. If you don't think I'm innocent, then stay out of it. I don't need your kind of help."

"Why didn't you tell me Terry and Jason were old friends?"

Chris rocked back a little on his heels. "What?" We were in our studio apartment over Gus's restaurant. He'd walked in after a long, hard day doing fall cleanups for his landscaping company. I hadn't even let him get all the way up the stairs.

"You heard me. Jason and Terry were thick as thieves until Terry went to prison. That's what they were, specifically. Thieves. At least that's what the Busman's Harbor PD believed."

Chris finished climbing the steps. He leaned against the little dining table where we ate, facing me. I was too keyed up to sit down. "How would I have known that?" he asked.

"He's your brother."

"I've explained this. I barely knew Terry when he was a young adult and I was a teenager. He went off to join the service when he was twenty. After he got out four years later, he basically never came home."

"Maybe not back to your cabin, but he was in town."

"He was around. I knew that. I'm pretty sure he saw

our aunt, our mom's sister. He may have even seen Cherie, but she and I didn't talk about him."

Cherie was the younger sister Chris had raised from the time he was in high school. After his dad had abandoned them, and then Terry had, and then his mom had gotten too sick and had gone away, too, he'd given up his own chance at college to stay home with her. It had been a terrible mess. The stress of his father's behavior and his mother's disease had blown his family apart. Chris's dad was in Florida, his mom in a nursing home there. Cherie lived in San Diego now. At least Chris thought she did. They never spoke. And Chris had only started visiting Terry in prison at the end of his sentence.

"I always believed Terry felt guilty about leaving me with Mom, who was obviously sick, and Cherie. And later just with Cherie. He could have contributed, financially, physically, emotionally, but he didn't." Chris paused. "The truth is, I didn't blame him. My dad adopted him and gave him his name, but he made it clear right along that Terry didn't belong in that house."

"You never went to visit him in prison."

"I wasn't angry that he left us, but I was furious that he robbed Hudson's and shot that kid. That clerk could have died. The truth is, I always looked up to Terry, but when he came back from the service, he was lost. I'd hear he was in town, then I'd hear he was in Portland or in Boston." Chris pushed off the table and stood up. "Once he was convicted, I wanted nothing to do with him."

"Until now."

Chris picked at a cuticle on a work-roughened hand. "I'm doing my best, Julia. He's my brother. I want us to be close, but it's hard. That's why I like being around your family so much. It's so easy."

There were plenty of times when it didn't feel easy

with my family. When you worked together and lived in the same small town and most of the money you lived on came out of the same pot, it wasn't easy. But it was nothing like what Chris had been through. Nothing.

"I'm not sure he even wants me to help him," I said. "He blatantly lied to me. This is a small town. Did he think I wouldn't find out?"

"He's panicking. He claims he was innocent last time," Chris protested. "Can you imagine the nightmare of being in the middle of something like this again?"

"He was inside Hudson's when Howland got there. So was the gun. He was convicted," I said.

Chris sighed, the long sigh of a man who understood the odds. "I'm sorry. I'm sorry I put you in this position. I don't know what else to do."

"I don't like being lied to."

"No one does. I'll talk to him, make him promise to be straight with you." He repeated, "I don't know what else to do."

Clearly he didn't. He was in a tough spot. He had reconnected with his brother, the only family member he was in touch with, and now he might lose him again. "I'm sorry I got mad," I said.

"I'm sorry you had a reason to get mad," he responded.

We were quiet for a moment.

"Did you find out anything today?" he asked. "Are there any other suspects?"

"Not much. Dmitri, the guy on the demo crew who didn't show up for work, is still missing. They all live together in a house Mark Cochran owns. Dmitri wasn't there the morning of the murder. Most of his stuff is cleared out."

"Well, that's something, isn't it?"

"I don't know. According to the kid on the crew who

speaks the most English, Dmitri kind of showed up out of the blue and attached himself to them. They don't seem surprised he left the same way."

"What about Pru?" he asked.

"It didn't seem right to go there pestering today. I'll go tomorrow."

"So you'll stay on it? Please?" He couldn't have looked more appealing.

"I'll stay on it. But you need to talk to Terry and tell him he has to level with me from here on or I'm done."

"I'll talk to him," Chris promised. "First thing in the morning."

Chapter Thirteen

Mom was in the kitchen when we got to her house for dinner. "Hot dogs and hamburgers on the grill," she said when we came in. "Who knows how many of these beautiful fall evenings we have left. We stopped at Hannaford on the way back from lunch in Damariscotta. I picked up potato salad, baked beans, and a salad in a bag."

Mom smiled, but her energy seemed low, as if her houseguests had finally worn her down. Except for two summers ago when I moved back to Busman's Harbor and stayed with her for the season, she had lived alone since my father died. She valued her privacy and her time. I knew she was thrilled to have Marguerite and Tallulah visit, and she'd be relieved when they left.

"Kitchen plates and stainless tonight," Mom said. "Not so much fuss. Chris, will you start the grill?"

"On it."

When I went through the swinging door into the dining room, Marguerite, Tallulah, and Wyatt were at the table, large sheets of architectural drawings laid out in front of them.

"You're looking at the plans for the renovation," I said. "What do you think?"

"These are the 'before' floor plans," Wyatt corrected. "The way Windsholme is today. We're trying to figure out how I missed the secret room."

"Intriguing." I approached the table and stood behind Marguerite.

"So interesting," she said. "To see the halls I wandered in life flattened into two dimensions." She moved her finger along the bedroom corridor. "The vagaries of childhood memory. Some of these places and rooms are so vivid to me. The master bedroom my mother occupied, the nursery where I slept with the other children, the hallway that connects them. But other spaces might as well be drawn with wavy lines and labeled 'Terra Ignito.' I don't think I ever entered many of these bedrooms. I have no memory of them at all."

Tallulah pointed to one. "Here be dragons."

"Exactly," Marguerite replied.

Wyatt squinted at the drawing of the second floor. "I see some of the problem. The bedroom next to this one is quite large. It's got its own bath on one side, and a closet on the wall that adjoins the hidden space. I think the governess's room was originally a dressing room for that bedroom, later opened to the nursery and turned into a nanny's room when it was needed." She paused. "Mark probably thought it was boxed-in eaves like I did when he did the detailed measurements."

"Will this throw off your design?" I asked.

"No. The outside measurements are fine. We've accounted for the total volume of the house, and the wall between the room and the nursery isn't structural." She shook her head. "I'm just concerned this happened, and whether there are any other mistakes. I'll speak to Mark about it tomorrow."

"Let's see the new plans," Marguerite said. "I'm ready."

Wyatt gathered up the "before" plans and took the plans for the renovation out of a tube. She laid the white sheets of paper on the table with a flourish. She guided Marguerite and Tallulah through the drawings I'd seen hundreds of times. I'd pictured the new rooms in my head, painted the walls, and mentally moved into the space.

Mom came into the room while Wyatt was talking. She stood fidgeting beside me, neither of us able to relax.

"It's lovely!" Marguerite clapped her hands. "I love what you've done with it. How practical it is for the business. How wonderful the residences are upstairs. It makes me so happy someone will be using the place again. That the Morrows will be living at Windsholme."

I breathed a deep sigh of relief. My mother owned Windsholme outright. Marguerite didn't get a say in what happened to it. But nonetheless, I'd cared deeply what Marguerite thought about our plans. She was the last living family link to the house as it had been.

Next to me. Mom seemed to relax as well, the tension and tiredness leaving her body. She cared what Marguerite thought, too. It was like the original Morrows were giving us permission, and without even realizing, we had been waiting for it.

Wyatt declined Mom's invitation to dinner, saying she had plans. Livvie and her family arrived. It was a casual gathering, full of side conversations about Page's day at school, Marguerite and Tallulah's trip to Pemaquid with Mom.

Mom thanked Sonny so lavishly for taking down the

porch screens that he blushed. It was a miserable job.
Almost as miserable as putting the warped old wooden
screens up in the spring. Nobody asked about my day,
which was probably just as well.

After dinner the Snugg sisters came over with a plate
of Vee's excellent brownies. Tallulah fetched the journal
and Marguerite's reading glasses. I bit into my brownie.
It had a slight crust on the top and was chewy on the
inside and so, so chocolaty. Despite the stresses and
tragedies of the week, in that moment I nearly passed out
from happiness.

Marguerite read.

"July 11, 1898

*"There's going to be a party! There is much
excitement in the household. Captain Beal and
the crew have sailed to Boston to pick up the
guests who will stay the weekend. Others will
arrive in their own yachts from points along the
Maine coast where they are summering.*

*"When the subject of the party first came up, I
was unsure what my role would be. Surely, I
would make a brief appearance with the young
men to say good night and that would be it. But
the less formal customs of the summer apply
here, too. Mrs. Morrow the younger invited me to
choose a dress from her wardrobe.*

*"I was happy to be invited, but unsure I could
find anything suitable. Mrs. Morrow is fifteen
years older than me and prefers to be fully
covered even in these hot days of summer. But
when I came to her room she had three ball
gowns laid out on the bed. They were all quite*

acceptable, more fashionable than I would have hoped. 'I won't be wearing any of these this summer,' she said. 'You may choose one for the party.'

"*I chose an ice-blue gown with flowers at the shoulders and yards of gauzy cloth that falls from the back to form a sort of cape. Mrs. Morrow says it was made for her in one of the best shops in Boston. It's too wide in the waist. Mrs. Morrow says Mrs. Franklin is good with a needle. If she is, it will be the first thing anyone has identified that she is good at. I wore my spectacles when I tried the gown on, so I could see myself, but I won't wear them to the party. This is my first ball gown and I intend to have a good time.*"

Marguerite stopped. "That's the end of the entry."

"Let's read one more," Fee suggested.

"Yes, please." Even Page was still interested, captured by the mention of a ball gown no doubt.

Marguerite looked ahead. "The next entry is short. Let's do it." She continued.

"July 15, 1898

"The house is all a flutter, cleaning, cooking, making beds, and moving furniture. There are so many guests the young men have moved back into the nursery so visitors can have their rooms. The yacht has returned and the guests are all about the place, playing croquet on the lawn, bathing at the little beach. Only Mr. Morrow doesn't participate. He is locked up in his study. The family fortune is made from ice. You would

*think the summer would be slow in the ice
business, with no rivers to harvest, but Mr.
Morrow says it is the busiest time, 'because it is
when ice is needed the most.'*

*"Indeed every day the little boat that comes
from Busman's Harbor to deliver groceries and
newspapers brings blocks of ice for the enormous
icebox in the kitchen. Mrs. Stout makes ice cream
or frozen custard almost every evening. She says
on the night of the ball we will have something
called baked Alaska. I cannot wait!*

*"There is a tension between Mr. Morrow and
Mr. Frederick, who is supposed to work for him,
but who hasn't left the island all summer. Mr.
Morrow fusses and fumes, but Mrs. Morrow
senior can always be counted upon to defend Mr.
Frederick. 'I prefer him to be here with me,' she
says, and that's the end of the discussion, until
the next time."*

Marguerite closed the journal. Sonny said, "Time
to go."

"But we didn't get to hear about the ball," Page
complained.

"It's a school night for fifth graders," Livvie said.
"Leave some for next time."

After they left, along with the Snugg sisters, Chris
and I helped with cleanup and prepared to go, too. I
found Marguerite alone in the living room when I went
to say good night.

"Julia, dear, can I ask you for something?"

"Of course."

"I would like to go out to Windsholme again, with
only you and Tallulah. It was wonderful having the

whole family there the other day, along with Wyatt and Mark, but I didn't feel I could linger. Wyatt's plans are beautiful and I am happy for your mother and your family you can do this, but I would like to say good-bye to the house I knew."

I hated to disappoint her. "I am so sorry, Marguerite. When I spoke to the state police detectives today, they didn't know when we'd be able to return to the island."

"Perhaps you could tell them I am a very old woman who must return to Boston in four days and who will never get a chance to see my childhood home again." She cocked her head with the pinned-up white braids to one side and steepled her hands in front of her in supplication. All she needed was a halo.

I laughed. "Does this work often for you, this very old woman thing?"

"Very often," she replied. "Let me know if you need my help with the police officers."

Chapter Fourteen

The next morning, to my surprise, when I called Lieutenant Binder, he gave me permission to take Marguerite and Tallulah to Morrow Island. The tale of my nonagenarian cousin bidding farewell to the old homestead moved him, exactly as the nonagenarian herself had predicted it would.

"When can the demo crew get back to work?" I asked Binder. "I'm getting pressure to get the job completed."

"Just a minute." He put me on hold and was gone longer than I expected. That was a change. When I'd seen him work before it had always been his case, his decision. He had the facts at hand and acted quickly. When he finally got back to me, he said, "Here's the deal. You go over to the island accompanied by Officer Dawes this morning. Our team will do one more search this afternoon. If we don't find anything, we'll give you the 'all clear' and the demo team can go back to work tomorrow."

"Why don't you go out this morning and be done with it?" I argued. "Then I can take my cousins to the

island in the afternoon and not tie up Officer Dawes."
Marguerite had made it clear she didn't want an en-
tourage.

Binder hesitated. "We can't go this morning because
we're waiting on dogs."

"Dogs?" So they were still looking for evidence.
Probably none of the various hatchets and tools they'd
taken from the island had been the murder weapon.

"Julia." The warning in his voice told me he'd said as
much as he was going to.

"Okay, be like that. But if you think there's a good
chance demo can resume tomorrow, I'd like to bring the
stuff in the sealed-off room back with us."

Another long hesitation, though this time he didn't
put me on hold. "Fine. As long as Officer Dawes inspects
everything you take."

"Deal. Thank you."

At Mom's house Tallulah and I got Marguerite bundled
up for the boat ride. Mom was at work at Linens and
Pantries. She'd gotten rid of most of her shifts for the
duration of her cousins' visit, but she couldn't trade them
all away. Her absence eliminated any awkwardness for
me about taking the trip to Morrow Island without her.

Jamie met us at the town pier where our Boston
Whaler was tied up. He seemed happy for the adventure,
glad to get out of whatever he was supposed to be doing
that morning.

During the ride, Marguerite sat in the back of the
boat, swaddled in blankets. Even Tallulah, the human
furnace, deigned to put on the leather jacket. As we neared
Morrow Island, I saw the young seal again, sitting on
the same rock outcropping. He followed us with his

big, round eyes as we glided past. "He looks so alone," I said.

"He is alone." Jamie cupped his hand around his mouth. "Hey, buddy! It's time to go south," he shouted. "Time for you to get underway."

The seal turned his head and followed our movement to the dock.

"Do you think we should check on him?" I asked when we'd tied up at the dock.

"Who? The seal? It's illegal to go within a hundred and fifty feet of him," Jamie answered. "Leave him alone. He knows what to do."

"Do you think he's sick?" Seals had washed up all along the Maine coast the previous year, dead from distemper.

Jamie thought a moment. "Has he moved from there?"

"I saw him dive into the water when I was on the *Jacquie II* the other day."

"He's feeding. He's fine," Jamie said. "Leave him be."

There was yellow crime scene tape around the woodpile. Lieutenant Binder had said not to go near it and I had no desire to. The thought of Jason lying there under the logs . . . I shuddered.

"You okay?" Jamie was good at noticing people and their reactions. His job demanded it.

"Yeah. Someone walked over my grave."

Jamie looked over at the woodpile. "Maybe not *your* grave."

I stared up the steep hill toward Windsholme and once again wondered how we'd get Marguerite up there. Reminding myself that she'd made it last time, I led our little group slowly up the path to the dining pavilion.

Jamie and Tallulah flanked Marguerite. She made good use of her cane and didn't hold on to either of them.

At the pavilion we stopped. Marguerite sat on a picnic bench while I gathered three large plastic bins to put the sealed room's furnishings in. The bins were normally used to store linens and paper goods—anything the mice would find attractive—over the winter. Morrow Island didn't have squirrels or even chipmunks, but we did have mice, voyagers no doubt on the hundreds of ships that had stopped at the island, both during my family's ownership and before. With constant access to seafood, Le Roi thought mousing was beneath him. The population was kept in check by the owls and hawks that visited and we never saw the mice in the summer. But once we were gone, the place shut down, the water turned off, the mice took over like they owned the place. It added a burden to spring cleaning, which was why anything that made good nesting material was sealed up, but other than that we lived with them in harmony, neither much interfering with the other.

We left the pavilion, this time with Tallulah and me flanking Marguerite on the path and Jamie carrying the tubs. When we reached Windsholme, Marguerite turned and started for the woods.

"The playhouse," she cried. "So many happy memories."

The path through the woods to the playhouse had become overgrown in the past year. A perfect, miniature replica of Windsholme, it had two good-sized rooms and had been used to house the island caretaker and his wife. Now it was unoccupied and rarely visited. With a limited crew and a lot of ground to tend, the landscape around it wasn't a priority. Marguerite, however, traveled on, moving low branches out of her way with her cane.

"Can we go inside?" she asked.

"Of course." I rushed around her to open the door. When I did the smell of mildew whooshed out. "I don't really think—" I started to say, worried about the state of a ninety-plus-year-old's pulmonary system.

Marguerite would not be deterred. She took two strides and was inside the playhouse. "The best thing about summers at Windsholme was the other children." She turned slowly, taking in the space. The front room had a stone fireplace, an old-fashioned kitchen counter with a sink in it, a small, round table, two hard wooden chairs, and a daybed that served as a couch. "I was my mother's only child," she said, "a widow's daughter, far too much the center of her attention. In the summers, my half brothers' children were here and we were allowed the run of the place. William had two sons and Charles a son and two daughters. I was the youngest; they were all older than me, and so tolerant of me tagging along. They were much more welcoming to me than the grown-ups were to my mother, the much younger, olive-skinned second wife. We played in the playhouse for hours." She stomped into the second room, the one we called the bunk room. Wooden bunk beds lined the two opposite walls. We'd removed the mattresses. They made the playhouse far too attractive to our high school and college-aged employees, who always seemed to pair up over the summer. None of us could follow her into the bunk room; the space left between the beds was too narrow.

"So many happy hours," we heard her say. "We played here, and on the little beach on the other side of the island, and hours and hours of croquet and badminton on the front lawn. I was too young to hit anything with a badminton racket, so my job was to retrieve the shuttlecock when someone missed it." She came to the doorway between the rooms. "They're all gone, now, of course. I'm the only one left."

We went to Windsholme after that. I worried Marguerite was down, but she was buoyed by the possibilities of the empty house with no demo crew or large group trailing behind her. This time we entered on the other side of the house, through the French doors to the west wing. I thought Marguerite would linger, but she moved as fast as her two legs and one cane could carry her. "This is where my half brothers played billiards after dinner. This is where my mother played the piano while the brothers and their wives played bridge."

We reentered through the dining room and went up the back stairs. Marguerite lingered in her mother's old room. "I better get to work on stuff in the secret room," I said.

Tallulah said, "I'll help you."

"Don't pack anything away until I get there," Jamie reminded me.

We left Marguerite alone with her thoughts and Jamie to watch her. I carried the plastic tubs across the scaffolding to the other side of the second floor.

The secret room was as we had left it, undisturbed for over a century, and apparently undisturbed for the last two days, despite the murder and presence of dozens of police and technicians on the island. Tallulah helped me photograph the entire space using my phone, pointing out items or angles I might have missed.

Now that I'd heard the entries from Lilly's journal

the room felt different. When I'd first seen it through
the framing, it was like a period room in a museum. A
place where time stood still. But now the room had
come alive. It belonged to a happy, adventurous young
woman who was having the summer of her life. What
could have happened here? Why was it left like this?

Lilly had written that Frederick Morrow's room had
a locked doorway into hers. That made sense if the room
had originally been, as Wyatt surmised, the dressing
room for his adjacent bedroom. A blank wall ran from
the end of the bed to the corner of the room nearest the
hallway. I felt the old plaster for a door frame, but it was
smooth.

I heard Marguerite coming toward us down the hall,
telling Jamie who had slept in each bedroom.

"How do you think your grandmother is doing with
all this?" I asked Tallulah.

"Fine. Fantastic. She's thrilled to be here."

Tallulah was an upbeat person. I worried she'd missed
some sign of distress. "Is she upset we're changing Windsholme so much?"

Tallulah was on the bed examining the books. "She
loves that the house will still be here and will be used."
Tallulah hesitated, as if looking for the right words. "You
don't need to worry about Granny being polite. You may
have noticed she says what she thinks, sometimes to
a fault."

We were both still chuckling at that when Marguerite
teetered into the nursery. "I slept here with the younger
children," she told Jamie. "Windsholme was the only
place I ever slept in a room with other children until I
went away to school. In the summer, when the days are

so long, we'd stay up giggling for hours. It was like summer camp for me."

"I know how that is." As a child Jamie had spent plenty of nights on Morrow Island, talking half the night with Livvie and me. "We need to get back," he said.

He helped Tallulah and I strip the room. We emptied the bureau, writing desk, and wardrobe. Then we removed the light summer bedspread, cotton blanket, and the yellowing sheets from the thin mattress, then rolled it up and took apart the bed frame. The writing desk, chair, nightstand, and bureau were light. We could easily take them in the Whaler. The old wardrobe was another story. Sonny and Chris would have to come for it later.

Marguerite watched our every move. Her eyes were bright, but her body sagged. It was time to get her home.

On our way down the hallway, I put down the bin I carried. "Wait a sec." I dashed into the bedroom that had been Frederick Morrow's. There was a small closet, and at the back of it, another door. I tried it, but it didn't budge. It had been closed off from the other side.

Leaving the island, we sailed by the seal. He tracked us with his eyes. "Go south," Jamie called to him again. "Go find the rest of your tribe."

Chapter Fifteen

I called Sonny from the Whaler on the way back and he met us at the pier with his pickup. I was glad to be able to offer Marguerite a ride back to Mom's house, though after she made a couple of unsuccessful attempts to climb in, he had to lift her into the cab.

Once we had settled Marguerite in with a cup of warm tea and a chicken salad sandwich, I went to Mom's garage and pulled out the Subaru. I'd loved my old Caprice, but a month earlier, it had announced loudly and definitively that it was through. At first, I was disappointed to lose a car with so much character as the old Caprice and trade it for the most common and therefore anonymous car in Maine. But then I experienced the miracle that when I turned the key the engine started, the heat came on, and the wipers cleaned the windshield. The Subaru and I began a love affair.

I could have walked to Pru's house, but I dreaded going there and wasn't ready to. Instead I drove to Thistle Island, where Emmy lived. The island was connected to the mainland by a swing bridge that pivoted open to let boats reach moorings up the river. Boat traffic was down in the waning days of the season. Every day, pleasure boats were being taken out of the water and buttoned up for winter storage. By this time of year, only the lobstermen used the narrow channel, so the bridge stayed closed and I traveled the road that ringed the island, reaching Emmy's trailer in twenty minutes.

Her trailer was parked on her grandmother's property. From the outside it looked worn, but inside Emmy had done her best to create a functional home for Vanessa and Luther. If her grandmother's house had been on a waterfront lot on the other side of the road, the land alone would have been worth a million dollars. What a difference two hundred yards made.

Emmy opened the door before I was even up the path. "What brings you out here this afternoon?" She gestured for me to come in.

Vanessa was still at school. Luther sat in a high chair pulled up to the trailer's single table.

"How are you doing?" I asked.

"Okay, I guess," she answered. "I'm freaked out Jason was murdered, like everyone else is, but really, I'm okay."

"You told me you were seeing him. I was worried—"

"I don't want you to think I'm cold. Of course, I'm upset. But my relationship with Jason was . . . I guess 'casual' is the best word for it. Ninety-nine percent of it took place at the Snowden Family Clambake, right under your nose."

"But I thought . . . I mean, you're both single adults."

She smiled. "Adults, yes. Single, hardly. I have two jobs and two kids at home. Jason had two jobs and two kids he spent time with. Our 'big affair' consisted of flirting at work and exactly two dates, a burger at Crowley's and one nice dinner at the Bellevue Inn. We had a romantic meal, and then I drove myself home and changed Luther's diaper."

"Your relationship drove Pru crazy."

"It did. At first I worried the only reason Jason was into me was to drive his ex crazy. But after he and I went out that second time, I got comfortable he was interested in me."

I hesitated. "You don't think Pru was angry enough to—"

Emmy's head snapped back. "Kill him? How can you even ask me that?"

"Someone killed him. Terry thinks the cops suspect him."

"That's ridiculous. Terry's the nicest guy. He always helped me. I didn't even have to ask."

"He's an ex-con. He had a fistfight with Jason the day before the murder. You can see how the cops might get there."

Emmy's big blue eyes opened wide. "Do *you* think Terry killed Jason?"

"Of course not," I answered. "But if not Terry or Pru, who could it have been? When you were with Jason did he mention anything he was into, anything at all that could have gotten him killed?"

"No." She hesitated.

"What?" When she didn't answer, I pressed her. "Emmy, come on. You don't want Terry to go back to jail, do you? If you know something, tell me."

"It's probably nothing."

"Anything at all might help."

Still, it took a while before she spoke. "When the weekday clambakes ended after Labor Day, I thought Jason and I would see more of each other. Instead, I saw him less. He would . . ." She stopped again. I waited as patiently as I could. Finally, she went on. "During the week, between clambakes, sometimes he would be gone for two or three nights. He'd drop out of sight, basically. He wouldn't be able to see me, but also he wouldn't call or text for days at a time. He didn't try to reach me and I couldn't reach him."

"Do you think it was another woman?" Maybe there was someone else. Someone we didn't know about who was close enough to kill.

"I did wonder," Emmy said. "I've explained how casual things were between us. There was certainly no agreement about or even discussion of exclusivity." Her brow puckered.

"But," I prompted.

"I don't think that was it. I never got the sense he was seeing someone else. But I could have read the situation wrong." She gave a little laugh. "I've done that before."

"Did you ever see Jason with any of the members of the demolition crew working at Windsholme?" I asked.

"I wouldn't know any of them if I passed them in the street. Do you think they had something to do with his murder?"

"Probably not. Do you know where Jason's money came from? That big, fancy new boat?"

"From lobstering." Emmy seemed amazed I had to ask. "He was a highliner. You know that."

Did I? If Jason was such hot stuff, why did he still make time to work at the clambake? "I'm sorry about Jason," I said.

"I'm sad," Emmy said. "I'm sad and I'm mad. I should have made more of an effort to spend time with him.

It might have been great. Life is too short, you know? Look at Jason. Life is too short."

There were cars in the driveway and along the street when I got to Pru Caraway's house. I wasn't surprised to spot Livvie's ancient minivan among them. Seeing Livvie's van made me feel terrible. How could I be coming here hoping to question this woman about her husband's murder? Pru had worked at the clambake for my parents, for Sonny when he'd run the business, and now for me. I should have planned to come as her employer.

I'd had enough presence of mind to stop at Gina's Farm Stand on the way back from Emmy's and pick up an apple pie, so at least I wasn't arriving empty-handed. I climbed out of the Subaru and picked the pie up off the seat.

Inside the house, Pru's living room was crowded with women. Livvie came to embrace me. "Pru will appreciate you coming."

"Where is she?"

"In the kitchen. Follow me."

Livvie headed toward the kitchen. Pru's house wasn't what I'd been expecting at all. From outside, it looked like its neighbors, a two-story house on a small in-town lot without a view. The houses on the street had been developed after World War II to provide affordable homes in what was then a thriving fishing port. I'd been in and out of these houses all through elementary and middle school for birthday parties and sleepovers. They were three bedrooms up, living, dining, kitchen down. Over the years, many of them had been altered to add a powder room downstairs, or a garage or a deck in the back.

Pru's house was something else. The living room was bright and cheery with aqua walls and fancy, gleaming woodwork that couldn't have been original. The furniture all matched, or rather the pieces complemented one another. The room felt like it was designed by someone who watched a lot of HGTV or who read articles in glossy decorating magazines with titles like "A Summer Retreat in Maine."

The kitchen was even more surprising, stocked with fancy stainless appliances and countertops made of some sort of bright, white composite with sparkly white stones embedded in it. The wall between the kitchen and dining room had been taken down to create one long room with sliding doors at the end that opened to a big deck. The white dining table near the sliders was laden with food—ham, turkey, potato salad, baked beans in a warming tray, fruit salad, and plenty of desserts. Livvie took my pie and put it on the table.

"Julia." Pru came forward to embrace me.

"I am so sorry." I hugged Pru back and felt her bony shoulders. Pru had always been thin, though now in middle age, she'd thickened through the middle. She and Jason were the living embodiment of the old complaint that men get handsomer with age and women get older. Her reddish brown hair had thinned. She never did anything with it except pull it back in a ponytail. I'd always seen her as a woman worked to the bone who didn't have time to care how she looked. But she obviously cared how her home looked.

"It's such a shock," Pru said. "But then it must have been for you, too. You found him."

"It was," I agreed.

Jason's son, Kirk, made his way into the kitchen and opened the shiny, double-doored refrigerator. He left a plate on the kitchen island while he poured cold soda into a plastic cup. He was about thirteen, round-shouldered and miserable. My father had died when I was twenty-five and I still wasn't over it. How could this poor kid cope?

"Thank you for coming," Pru said to me. "Please stay and eat something."

I fixed myself a plate of food, ham, potato salad, baked beans, and bread and butter pickles, and sat in the living room with Livvie and Pru's friends. A huge television dominated the room. Various gaming devices sat on a shelf below it. The leather couch was so new it still smelled like a baseball glove. The women in the room were lobstermen's wives, all married with children. Being with them reminded me how out of step I was. I picked up my plate and went out to the deck.

There were half a dozen women deep in conversation crowded on the built-in benches at one end of the deck. At the other end a lone woman sat eating at the picnic table.

"I'm Julia." I sat down across from her.

"Aggie," the woman said. "Pru's sister."

Once she said it, I caught the resemblance. Aggie had the same sharp nose, round eyes, high forehead and wavy hair, though Aggie's was shot through with gray.

"I'm sorry for your loss," I said.

"Not my loss." She glanced at the women at the other end of the deck to make sure no one was listening. "I never liked the man. But I feel bad for my sister and the kids."

Her admission startled me. People so rarely said something negative about the recently deceased, especially to a stranger. Her frankness made me bold. "Why didn't you like him?"

"He was a petty thief and general jerk when he and Pru first got together. And though he backed away from that life eventually, there were the other women."

"While he and Pru were married?"

Aggie didn't waver. "While they were dating, engaged, married, divorced. It never stopped. That man was a continuous flirt. Women, men, animals, if it had a pulse he'd flirt with it. He could make you feel like the most special person in the world, but really it was all about him and his ego. He needed you to find him charming. Sometimes, with women, it went too far. At least a few times a year."

"Is that why he and Pru divorced?"

"Yes. She ignored it for as long as she could, but then she was done with him."

"She must still have had feelings," I said. "She seemed jealous of a woman Jason was seeing this summer."

Aggie put down her fork and offered the blunt response I'd already come to expect from her. "If you're asking me if my sister killed her ex-husband, the answer is no."

"How can you be sure?"

"I would love to tell you it's because I know my sister and she is the salt of the earth. She is not. Like all of us, she has issues, though I don't believe she could murder anyone in cold blood, much less the father of her kids. But the reason I'm sure is that fancy car over there." Aggie pointed with her chin to the end of the driveway where a gigantic, black, late-model SUV sat parked. "She's not going to kill the goose who lays the golden eggs."

"Jason bought that?" In addition to Jason's lobster boat, there were the new appliances in the updated kitchen, the new furniture and tech in the living room, and this expensive vehicle. Pru worked long hours at the clambake during the season, where we didn't pay her enough, and in the cafeteria at the high school where she was similarly poorly paid. Unless Pru had a hidden source of income, Jason must have paid for all of it.

"He did. For the first three years after the divorce he was constantly behind on child support, and didn't put a dime into this house, which he still half owned. But something changed the last couple of years. Nothing was too good for his kids or his house. He's been pouring money into it. It made Pru so happy, and after everything she put up with all these years, she deserved it."

"Where do you think all this money came from?" I asked.

"Lobstering, I assume. You know, landings have been way up these last few years. Jason upped his license, dropped more traps. It's a boom and bust business, but mostly boom lately."

I was skeptical that Jason's fortune could turn around in two years entirely from lobstering. It was true the last couple of seasons had been record breakers, but as any lobsterman would tell you, when the catch was high, the prices were low, and when the prices were high, lobsters were scarce. It was a simple matter of supply and demand.

There didn't seem like much to say after that. I said good-bye and told Aggie it was nice to meet her. Pru was in the living room. I gave her another hug on my way out. This wasn't a day to have a private conversation.

Livvie walked me to the door. "Did you ask Pru why she didn't come to work on Monday?" I said when we reached the front porch.

"I didn't even have to bring it up. First thing when she saw me she apologized up and down. She said Kirk was sick."

"Kirk is a teenager. Pru would only have stayed home with him if he was really ill." Kirk had looked healthy if sorrowful in the kitchen half an hour earlier.

"Yeah," Livvie agreed. "Pru hardly ever missed a day of work before, but when she did she always called to let me know."

Chapter Sixteen

When I left Pru's I went to Gus's and parked in the little lot behind the kitchen door. Gus didn't like me leaving my car there. "Parking's scarce enough in this town. Leave it for the paying customers." It was three o'clock, closing time, so I didn't think he'd mind too much if I was only there for a few minutes.

I entered through the kitchen, passing the passage to the walk-in refrigerator and the stairs to my apartment. Gus was cleaning behind the counter. The front room of the restaurant was deserted.

"I left my car out back," I told him as I poured the last of a pot of coffee into one of his white mugs.

"See you move it when you're done," Gus responded.

"I will. Is Bard here?"

"Ayup. In the dining room."

From the front room I passed through the archway to the dining room. At the back of the otherwise empty room Sonny's dad, Bard Ramsey, held court as he did most days. Bard had been a highliner, the label for a highly successful fisherman, or in his case lobsterman. But now that he was in his seventies, the hard physical work had taken a toll on his shoulders and hips, and he only went out when one of his sons, Sonny or Kyle, was available to help.

In the afternoons he went to Gus's. He sat with the other old lobstermen. Some of them were retired, some semiretired like Bard, and some still pulled a full complement of traps before they arrived at Gus's. Lobstering might seem like a solitary occupation, long hours alone on a boat, but the truth was most lobstermen chatted all day, either to the sternman—who was the assistant who baited the traps, threw the seaweed and miscellaneous creatures they caught back into the sea, and generally did the dirtiest of the dirty work—or over the radio to other lobstermen out on their boats. They had talked all their lives and they were still talking.

"Darlin', happy to see ya." Bard greeted me as I approached their table. The other men put down their forks or their coffee cups and stared openly. It wasn't often they were interrupted.

"Hey, Bard. I have a quick question for you," I called to him.

"Sit down, sit down." Without rising he pulled a chair from the table behind him and squeezed it in next to him.

I sat down, lowering my coffee mug to the table. "I've been thinking about Jason Caraway's boat," I said.

One of the men whistled. "That's a Cadillac of the Sea, that one."

The others nodded their agreement.

"Decked out."

"She's a corkah, all right."

"Spared no expense."

This was the way lobstermen described boats they admired.

"Were you wondering what will happen to it?" Bard

rubbed a beefy hand across his grizzled chin. He'd gotten spotty on shaving in his semiretirement and patches of white whiskers showed here and there. "I imagine his kids will sell it once it gets through probate." He turned to the table. "One of you lads should buy it."

That brought hoots and hollers.

"Still payin' on the last one."

"Only way I'd buy it is if it would take itself out in the harbor and haul the traps without me."

"You'd don't think that's comin'? Robots will have us all out of work soon."

"Sooner than that global warming?"

More laughter. Lobstermen were great observers of the weather, far more sensitive to minor changes in the ecosystem than most, and they were strong guardians of the lobster fishery, which had sustained itself long after many fish stocks had collapsed. But they were often skeptical of scientists who made pronouncements from the comfort of their offices and labs. After all, some of those same scientists had been predicting the demise of the lobster industry for decades, through the last few years of record catches. But the lobster fishery had collapsed further south in Rhode Island and Long Island, where warm water had brought shell disease, and then the lobsters had all but disappeared.

The truth was the lobsters' life cycle was so obscure and complex neither side had the whole story. Each could have offered a lot to the other, though those dialogues rarely took place.

I attempted to get them back on track. "I was wondering about the *Money Honey*, because it's pretty new and looks really expensive."

"Ayup," Bard agreed.

"The thing is, was Jason a highliner? The boat and the man, do they match?"

This time it was Bard who led the guffaws. "Jason Caraway a highliner? He was a dub if ever there was." "Dub" was the word for a poor or inefficient lobsterman. One who used a lot of bait and fuel to find a small number of lobsters.

"But the boat," I said. "Is it possible for a lobsterman to get better?"

"Sure, sure," Bard answered. "Maybe he'd come into better places to put his traps because someone retired. And you do develop more knowledge as you go, a better understanding of where the little devils hide. But it's mostly instinct. I can usually tell within a season if someone's got it or not. If you don't know how to read the bottom, you're not going to improve much."

"Then where do you think Jason got the money for the boat?" They must have speculated about it. Not much got by these guys.

"Probably borrowed up to his neck," one of the men said.

"Secured by what? Would you loan him that kind of money?" someone else said. "I wouldn't."

"I heard Pru's parents have money and they paid," another said.

"I heard he came into some money when his dad passed away."

"No. He told me directly he invested in a business, a lobster processing plant Down East that paid out big when they sold it."

They all looked at one another, amused.

"Did anyone ask Jason directly?"

"Ha, ha, ha. Yeah, probably the IRS." More laughter.

"Or the DEA." There was more laughter, but then the table quieted. Drug smuggling wasn't funny.

"Did you ever hear that Jason was making money off drugs?" I asked.

The men around the table remained silent. It was an obvious question, something I'd wondered about every time Jason had brought that big boat to Morrow Island. Running drugs from Canada did happen. Not so long ago, he might have been moving cheap prescription drugs for altruistic reasons, as Chris had done. Now, most often, it was the worst of the worst. Fentanyl shipped from China to Canada and then smuggled across the border on boats big and small.

The opioid epidemic had devastated the lobstering community as it had rural communities everywhere. Help-wanted ads for sternmen said, "No druggies." Or, "I run a drug-free boat," hoping to attract those who didn't want to work with addicts. It had hit close to home for some of them. Bard's son Kyle had been addicted to prescription opioids. He was clean now and working, but it had to be a constant source of worry.

"Anyone ever heard Jason Caraway was moving drugs?" Bard asked the men directly.

To a person, they shook their heads. If Jason had been involved with drugs there would have been rumors. The men at that table would have heard them, for sure.

"Anythin' else?" Bard asked me.

I took my cue. "No. Thanks for your time."

I'd left my phone in my car. My screen showed a message. Sergeant Flynn.

"Julia, it's Tom Flynn. The lieutenant asked me to let you know we're done on the island. You're cleared to send your workmen back tomorrow and to have your clambake on Saturday."

Good news at last. Did it mean the dogs hadn't found anything, or did it mean they had?

I decided to head to Mark Cochran's office. He'd be the best person to tell the crew to return to work. Besides, I wanted to talk to him anyway.

I drove to Mark's office, which was about halfway up the two-lane highway that ran from busy Route 1 down to the harbor. During the design and contracting process, I'd loved going to meetings there. The building was gorgeous, crisply shingled on the outside, sleek and modern on the inside. It was intended to telegraph to potential clients, "I can build your multimillion-dollar waterfront home and it will be as wonderful as this office." It worked.

Mark's receptionist, who looked like he was a teenager, greeted me by name and offered coffee or water. Windsholme wasn't my property and it wasn't being renovated with my money, but Mom had included Livvie, Sonny, and me in every decision she'd made and everyone at Cochran Builders knew it. The receptionist told me Mark was finishing up a meeting and could see me shortly.

I said I'd help myself to water and went to get it. The office kitchen made me feel so good with its cherry cabinets and stone countertops. I sighed happily and looked at the samples stored in the room. Someday Windsholme would have three beautiful kitchens, an enormous one for catering functions and two small ones in Mom's and my living spaces. I'd initially been opposed to spending the money to renovate the house. Now that it was underway I found myself daydreaming about life on the island a lot.

I heard voices and the sound of the outer door opening and closing and then Mark appeared. "Sorry you had to wait, Julia. Did we have an appointment?"

"No. Sorry. I came to tell you the police have given permission for the demo crew to resume work on the island."

"That's great news." He beamed.

"Have you worked with the crew a lot?"

He nodded. "Yes. For several years now. They follow instructions well, are reliable, come in and get the job done for a steep but fair price." He relaxed, leaning back against the big island in their display kitchen. "I wasn't sure they'd take your job. Working on an island adds complexity to everything. I do all the hauling, dropping the dumpsters, arranging the pickups and disposal of the materials. But they still have to commute by boat and are stuck on the island all day."

"I'm glad they said yes. It probably helped that you could offer them housing."

"Housing is so difficult around here, especially during the season, I have to offer it to workers or I'd never get any to come here. Once the demo crew moves on I'll start renovating that house. It will be a good winter project to keep my employees busy."

And you'll sell it for a bundle when you're done. "The other day, in the sealed-off room, we spoke to two guys on the Russian crew."

"Joe and Dmitri. I like to bring Dmitri into conversations with clients because English is his first language. He picks up a lot more of the nuance."

"He's disappeared."

"So I've heard." Mark didn't seem concerned. "I can't say I'm surprised. Dmitri only joined the crew a few months ago. Apparently he appeared out of nowhere and it seems he disappeared the same way." Mark had been given the same story I had. "There's another reason I'm not surprised he's gone."

"What's that?" I asked.

"Dmitri didn't know a thing about demo work. I watched him on his first day on another of my jobs. It was like he'd never held a sledgehammer before."

I had a lot to think about as I drove back down the peninsula to town. What had I learned?

I'd learned that Terry and Jason had been friends before Terry went to prison. More than friends, they'd been partners in crime. Terry absolutely denied any relationship between the men in the present, aside from working together at the clambake and their mutual interest in Emmy. Jason's prior life of crime lent an interesting wrinkle to all the money he'd lavished on himself, Pru, and the kids—the fancy boat, the SUV, the improvements in the house. The money could have come from lobstering, but after my conversation with Bard and his cronies I doubted it. So where had it come from? What was Jason up to?

I was bothered by Dmitri's disappearance the day of the murder, though I was the only one who was. Mark Cochran and the other members of the demo crew didn't think it the slightest bit unusual. The look that had passed between Jason and Dmitri on the island haunted me. Each man seemed to signal, "I know something about you." Had Jason known something about Dmitri that got him killed?

Then there was Pru. I hadn't talked to her, but I thought her sister's argument about the golden goose was pretty compelling. Even if Jason had life insurance, could it possibly be worth more money than a live lobsterman buying gifts with his profits? And Jason was her kids' father. Pru had been nervous and petty and jealous from the moment Jason's flirtation with Emmy started, but her reputation around town was as a good mother and a hard worker. The latter was certainly true, and I had no reason to doubt the former. I did, however, have reason to doubt her excuse for not showing up for work on the day of Jason's murder. Had someone warned her to stay away?

And finally there was Terry. Terry had lied about his earlier relationship with Jason. What else was he lying about? He'd been off somewhere on the *Dark Lady* the morning of the murder. And while I was convinced he hadn't showed up for work because he believed he was fired, it sure didn't look good.

I'd learned a lot, but I hadn't gotten anywhere. I didn't have anything I could take to the police, who were undoubtedly ahead of me in many areas, like looking into Jason's finances.

The sun was low in the sky, casting long shadows when I left my car in Mom's garage and hiked the short distance over the harbor hill to my apartment. Gus would be gone, the building empty. It was a peaceful time of day I enjoyed, especially in the quiet period when the days the clambake ran were dwindling and our winter restaurant, Gus's Too, hadn't started up yet.

When I reached the familiar building, perched on pilings on a boulder over the harbor, I walked down the steep driveway to the little parking lot and toward the kitchen door, the one I had a key to, the one we used every day.

I was at the door, turning the key in the lock, when I heard a voice. "Excuse me, missus."

I jumped, turning toward the source of the sound. Alex, the young man on the demo crew, came toward me. I took a breath, my heart rate slowing. He didn't look aggressive. In fact, he looked the opposite, like he was sorry for bothering me.

"Could we talk for a little time?" he asked.

"Of course. What's the matter? Has Dmitri turned up?"

Alex shook his head. "No. This is why I'm talking here to you now. He has not returned and I am scared for him."

That was a change. I turned the key in the lock. "Come in."

He followed me into the restaurant, looking all around, at the kitchen, the booths, even the ceiling. "I have never been here before."

I wasn't surprised. Gus's was strictly for locals. There were no signs outside, and if he didn't know you, or you didn't arrive with someone he knew, you would be informed the place was full, no matter how much your eyes told you it was not. It was arbitrary and discriminatory, not to mention a terrible business practice, but it was also a refuge for the locals during the tourist season where they could drop their fake smiles and Old Salt facades.

"How did you know I lived here?" I said to him.

He flushed. "I asked the first person I met in the street."

Ah, the joy of small towns, particularly as the season wound down. People who would never enter their own addresses on a Web site were perfectly happy to point a stranger in the direction of someone's home in the real world. It came, I knew, from being stopped a half dozen times on a short walk during the summer by people asking directions. Despite all the Maine jokes about "You can't get theah from heah," folks were helpful 99 percent of the time. That tourist was probably headed to a cottage where he paid rent, or to a store to buy something, or to a restaurant to eat, all of them owned by locals.

"Can I get you something to drink, coffee, tea, water?" I asked.

Alex swallowed hard, the big Adam's apple bobbing. "No. I will not be staying long. Joe will wonder where I have gone."

Why did Joe care where Alex was during his time off? Didn't everyone need to get away from time to time? The forced company felt oppressive.

"I want to tell you I am concerned about Dmitri." Alex's face was solemn and determined, his mouth set.

I sat down on a stool at the counter. He did the same, leaving one stool between us. "You said you weren't surprised Dmitri left."

"That is what our boss told me to say. I have said it to you, to Mr. Cochran, and even to the police. But telling the truth, I am very worried about Dmitri." I didn't respond and he continued. "Joe is a good boss because we always have work and we are paid on time and fairly. But, in return, he doesn't like anyone to question what he does." He cleared his throat and went on. "Plus, because we are working with him and he is in charge of us, Joe likes to know where we are and what we are doing. Right now, he thinks I am at the store buying milk. He would not like me talking to you, especially about this. But Dmitri never told Joe where he was going. He disappeared all the time, most often for a few hours but sometimes for a day or more. Caused much aggravation. I think Joe would have fired Dmitri, except he needed him to translate. My English is not so good yet."

"Your English is great. How did the police respond when you told them you weren't surprised Dmitri had disappeared?"

Alex leaned on the counter, skinny forearms bent toward his face. "They did not react to anything I told them. There were two policemen, one bald and one who looked like a soldier. They sat there like this the whole time." Alex pulled his mouth into a straight line and stared at me, unblinking, with a gaze that conveyed deep skepticism.

I laughed in spite of the seriousness of the subject and the risk he was taking by talking to me. "That's Lieutenant Binder and Sergeant Flynn. Don't let them put you off. They're like that with everyone."

He didn't believe me. "You too?"

"Well, maybe not me because they know me, but yes, in the beginning they were as you say, and they intimidated me. But you can't let them. If you're worried about Dmitri you have to tell them."

"No!" Alex was plainly horrified. "I cannot. I could lose my job, and if I lose my job I lose my work permit, and if I lose my work permit—" He stopped abruptly. The outcome was unthinkable. He took a deep breath. "I can tell you have some interest in this murder, beyond that it happened on your property. You didn't come to talk to us yesterday to see how we are feeling. I will talk to you, and I will tell you anything I hear, but I will not talk to the police."

"Alex, if I tell the police what you've told me, or anything you tell me in the future, they are going to want to talk to you. It's unavoidable."

He laid his hands, open, palms up on the counter. "Then you will have to be clever," he said. "If I find out anything the police need to know, you will have to be very, very clever how you tell them."

Chapter Seventeen

Chris came home and showered before we headed to Mom's for dinner. "How did the rest of your day go?" he asked.

"Interesting."

"Interesting, like helpful?"

I let out a long breath. "No. Interesting only like interesting." I walked him through my day.

When I got to my conversation with Alex, he stopped me. "I don't like the sound of this."

"It's not different than any of the other nosing around. Nosing around you asked me to do, for the record."

Chris glanced back over his shoulder. "For my permanent record?"

I laughed and the mood in the room lightened. "For the permanent record of our relationship, scattered with checkmarks for every time I was right."

He grabbed his jacket. "I don't even want to see it."

"I get double checkmarks whenever I'm right and I don't say, 'I told you so.'"

He groaned. "Now I know I don't. Never, ever."

He swept me into his arms for a kiss. "Thank you for helping Terry."

"Don't thank me yet."

"Thank you for trying."

Mom was cooking, ordinarily the three scariest words in the English language. My mother had been brought up by a succession of housekeepers who had left her with a scattershot set of cooking skills across several ethnic cuisines. Fortunately, the German housekeeper had taught her to make a delicious pot roast, which had entered Mom's limited rotation of company meals.

She had prepared the meat the day before because of her shift at Linens and Pantries. "Always better the second day," she said as she whipped potatoes. Five of the best words in the English language.

Livvie's family and the Snugg sisters arrived and we all dug into the pot roast, gravy, potatoes, and coleslaw. The foods beautifully complemented one another with their sweet and sour tastes. You could cut the meat with your fork.

Jason's murder did come up during the meal, but Mom quickly changed the subject. At last the plates were cleared and we got down to the business of why we were really there.

Tallulah brought the journal. Marguerite cleared her throat and read.

"July 17, 1898
  "A most unexpected and terrible thing has happened. The evening of the ball was all I hoped for. The dinner was sumptuous, a fish and a meat course, all followed by the delicious

baked Alaska dessert. The main parlor and great hall had been cleared for dancing and there was an orchestra.

"I would have been happy to stay in the background and watch, though I regretted leaving my spectacles off as everyone on the other side of the room was a colorful blur. My wish to be a spectator was not granted. I was asked to dance time and again. I was barely able to catch my breath and have some punch. Most of the other ladies were drinking champagne, the men something stronger. But my family has always been temperance and I was already so far from my usual daily activities, I declined.

"Mr. Frederick danced with me three times in the course of the evening. Each time he was more inebriated—and bolder, holding me too close and whispering indecent ideas into my ear. We whirled by Captain Beal standing to the side, looking resplendent in a uniform Mr. Morrow has made for his yachting crew. I tried to signal I needed rescue, but he seemed not to see.

"After our third dance, Mr. Frederick left me with some other ladies and I decided it was time to withdraw. I worried he would approach me again and I didn't want the evening spoilt. I didn't say good night, but quietly crept up the stairs. I could thank the Morrows the next day. I went through the nursery where William and Charles were already asleep, and closed my door. I dressed for bed and settled in to read. I could hear the music from downstairs, but faintly. It was pleasant and I was happy.

"Slowly, the evening came to an end. The music stopped. Conversations from the great lawn floated through my high window as the guests who were returning to their yachts said their good-byes. Footsteps came up the stairs to the bedrooms. I blew out my lamp and went to sleep.

"Then, in the night, I was awakened by the tumble of a lock, the turn of a latch."

Marguerite stopped reading, though she didn't close the book. She caught Sonny's eye, then looked meaningfully at Page.

"Page, go watch TV," Sonny said.

"But it's a school night." Page was a greater stickler for the rules than her parents.

"Go," Sonny commanded. "You heard the part about the ball. That's what you were here for."

"Aw, man."

My mother's only television was in the sitting room off her bedroom, a converted sleeping porch. We waited until we heard Page's footsteps tread up the stairs, and then Sonny signaled Marguerite to resume.

"Then, in the night, I was awakened by the tumble of a lock, the turn of a latch. A door burst open. It was not one of the young men from the nursery looking for me, but the other door to my room. Mr. Frederick charged in, staggering and calling my name. 'Lilly, Lilly, darling, I need you!'

"Before I could move he came to my bed. He tore the bedclothes from my clutched hands. He lifted my nightgown and touched me

*roughly. I had no doubt what he intended. I
screamed as loud as I could. He had his
breeches lowered and he . . . I cannot even
write it here. I kept up screaming though he
tried to cover my mouth with his hand. I will
never forget the feel of his hot, drunken breath
on my face.*

*"The door from the nursery banged open and
young Charles stood frozen in the darkness, but
only for seconds. He set upon his uncle, jumping
on his back, pummeling him and shouting.*

*"It seemed to go on forever, though surely it
was but a minute. The lamps were lit in the
nursery and the whole family was there and a few
of the guests. Frederick lurched away. My
nightgown was by this point on the floor. I
covered myself as best I could.*

*"'Frederick, go to your room,' Mrs. Morrow
senior commanded. 'You are drunk. The rest of
you disperse.'*

*"Charles was crying and plainly terrified. His
mother led him away. The doorway was empty
except for the senior Mrs. Morrow. 'I'll leave you
to your shame,' she said. 'Next time you lead a
wealthy man on, do not change your mind once
you have what it is you sought.'*

*"She left, closing the door, leaving me sobbing
in the bed."*

Marguerite looked up. "That's the end of the entry."
"You can't leave us here," Mom said. There were nods
around the table.

"You can't," Vee agreed.

Marguerite turned the remaining pages. "There are only a few left."

"Go on," Mom said. "Finish it."

Marguerite read.

"August 8, 1898

"I have not written in a long time. I thought I would be asked to leave, but the household goes on as if nothing has happened, except the porter has nailed the door between my room and Mr. Frederick's shut.

"I cannot forget as they all do so easily. I cannot forget and neither can young Charles, who is always solicitous of me. The rest of the time he is quiet and even more withdrawn than when we arrived. The summer in which I thought he would bloom has become a nightmare for him as it has for me.

"I maintain my composure during lessons with William and Charles. It is my happiest time of the day, though we always do our work in the nursery now, not around the island. The rest of the time I am sad and far away, like I am no longer in my own body. I am given to bouts of crying, which come unbidden and uncontrollable. I never know when the tears will come and it keeps me away from the family. When they think of me, which I believe is rarely, they have adopted Mrs. Morrow senior's fiction that I attempted to seduce Mr. Frederick. I have taken to eating all my meals with the servants. When I see Mr. Frederick I am sick to my

stomach and at heart. After the ball, he finally went back to Boston with Mr. Morrow to their offices. He was gone for some days and I'd begun to feel better, but now he is back and the feeling of utter helplessness has returned. Every night when I go to bed I feel his hands upon me once more.

"Mrs. Stout found me in the rose garden today, bawling like a washerwoman. She put her arms around me and said, 'You poor girl.' Her sympathy only made me cry harder. 'You should go home, girl,' she said. 'There is nothing for you here but pain. There is no shame in it.'

"But I can't bear the thought. What will I tell my family? How will I explain I have lost my position? Will I ever work again? I doubt the Morrows will give me a good reference. They will not want the tale spread, though I will never tell a soul.

"Can I ever marry now? It was by no means a certainty, but I always hoped. Those hopes have gone.

"In the late afternoon, when the family gathers on the porch and I know Mr. Frederick is with them, I walk over the top of the island on the path to the beach. There is a boulder there that hangs out over the water. I stand there and stare into the blue, blue of the channel. It isn't wide. In my swimming costume I could probably make it as far as the other side. Westclaw Point, it's called. But if I were to leap, in my shirt and boots and petticoats, I am certain I would die. I think

*about it all the time. They say it's not a bad
way to—"*

Marguerite closed the journal with a sharp *thwack*.

"That's it?" Livvie was appalled.

"That's all there is," Marguerite confirmed. "It goes
to the last line on the last page of the notebook."

"Do you think she went through with it?" Tallulah
asked. "Drowned herself. Is that why they sealed up
her room?"

"I expect they felt guilty," Mom said. "They pretended it was her fault, but they knew what had really
happened. Perhaps they couldn't face the room. They
needed it to disappear."

"They would have told her family some story about a
swimming mishap," Fee said.

"Now we're wildly speculating," Livvie objected.
"We don't know any such thing."

"You're right," Tallulah said. "We don't know. Maybe
she was fine. Maybe she worked out the summer and
went home."

We sat in silence for a moment. The candles had
burned down. I got up and flicked on the lights. Marguerite sat, a deep sadness in her hooded brown eyes.
It had been like fiction for us, a tale of distant people.
But her father, Lemuel, had, to all indications, partici-
pated in the charade that left a vulnerable young woman
scarred and alone. Though Marguerite had no memory
of Lemuel, who had died when she was a year old, it
must have affected her. And she had known her half
brothers, William and Charles.

"I want to know what happened," Tallulah said. "I can't stand this."

"Me too," I agreed. "But how?"

"We start on the Internet," Tallulah said.

"You won't have much luck with Smythe," I said, "even spelled that way. But it's the right place to begin."

Chapter Eighteen

I woke up in the morning determined to go back to Pru's. If Jason had unexplained sources of money it was likely to be at the root of his murder. Far more likely than Terry killing him over a petty jealousy about Emmy or a beef about a long-abandoned friendship. If anyone knew where Jason's money came from it was Pru.

I was relieved to see no cars parked on the street as I approached Pru's house on foot. The hulking, black SUV was in place at the end of the driveway, which meant she was probably home. I wondered if the Caraway kids would have gone back to school. The medical examiner hadn't released Jason's body. No funeral had been announced. The kids would have wanted to be out of the house and with their friends. Pru was a good mother and would have wanted a return to some kind of routine.

I climbed the front steps and rang the bell. After a few moments Pru opened the door. She wore a shapeless dress. Her hair was hidden by a kerchief and she had deep circles under her eyes. "Julia."

"Hello, Pru. I wonder if I could come in."

"Sure." She gave me a curious look, backed up so I could enter, and led me to her big new kitchen.

The living room, dining room, and kitchen were spotless. The other lobstermen's wives would never have left her with a mess to clean up. "What can I do for you?" She sat at the dining room table in front of the sliding doors to the deck.

She didn't offer me anything to drink, but I could hardly blame her. She looked terrible. I was the intruder. I sat across from her. "Are the kids here?"

"I sent them to my sister's. I hope their cousins can distract them. They were getting pretty antsy sitting around here and I couldn't cope." She pulled a cigarette from an open pack but didn't light it. "I quit seven years ago. The urge was gone until all this happened." She ran her fingers down the length of the cigarette. "I pull them out and stare at them."

"Don't do it." I meant it as a caution, not a nag.

She seemed to take it the right way and returned the cigarette to the pack. "I couldn't stand the kids bugging me about it. That's what got me to quit the last time. What do you want?"

It was a reasonable question. She knew I wasn't there to offer my support. She had closer friends and a sister for that. "I want to ask some questions about Jason."

"You're helping that Terry Durand." She said it as if it was a fact, not an accusation.

"Trying to."

"The police asked me directly if I thought he did it. They worked up to it. Did Jason have any enemies and so on. I didn't name Terry, but they already knew about him and they asked me."

"What did you tell them?"

"I said I didn't know. That Terry and Jason had history. And, of course, Terry had been in prison. He'd already shot someone. How much more of a step is killing a person?"

"You knew Terry and Jason were friends."

"Of course. Buddies. When I first took up with Jason they were hanging around together and for years after that. I never liked Terry. I thought he was bad for Jason. Got him into trouble."

"I heard they broke into summer places."

Pru worked a hand over the kerchief on her head. "If they did, I never saw any of what they got."

"Do you know why they fell out?"

"Jason was a married man with kids. He needed to grow up and take responsibility. Terry went to prison. Not much in common." Almost exactly what Howland had said.

"And when Terry got out?"

"I'm sure it was awkward for both of them. And then you went and hired Terry for the same job on the same tiny island."

I waited a moment before I added, "And they both seemed to have a weird thing for Emmy."

"Two middle-aged men showing an interest in a pretty young woman? That is not a 'weird thing' in my experience." Pru took the cigarette out of the pack again. I thought she might light it, but she didn't.

I smiled. "No, I guess it's not weird. You and Jason had been divorced for a while, but Jason's flirtation with Emmy did seem to bother you."

"Flirtation? Is that what we're calling it now? Believe me, no part of our divorce was more of a relief to me than that Jason's sex life was no longer my concern. That man sent me to Hades and back for more than a decade. Not only wasn't he faithful, he wasn't a good provider. Or at least I can say little of what he made found its way home. Perhaps that's more accurate. But the last two years, things had really changed. He fixed up the house, bought me a car. It wasn't completely unselfish, mind you. He said he wanted the best for his kids, but he still owns half the house. Any improvement he'll eventually get out of it." She stopped dead. "Owned. He still *owned* half the house." She paused. "And then that woman thought she was going to waltz in with her two brats and take what was owed me. Just because Jason started making real money after our divorce doesn't mean I didn't deserve it. I earned every penny that came my way."

Emmy had said her relationship with Jason was casual. Pru thought Emmy and her kids were going to live off Jason's money. "Emmy told me she and Jason weren't serious. They went out a couple of times," I said.

"Hah!" Pru snorted. "That's a lie. She was meeting him secretly on his boat. Sleeping with him there. There was plenty of hanky-panky on the *Money Honey*, I can tell you."

"You saw them?"

"No, no, no. After the storm last week I wanted to check on the boat. I knew Jason had made it back to port in the nick of time, because he had the grace to call and tell me and the kids he was okay. After the storm, I called him and called him. No answer, which wasn't unusual. Another reason I'm glad he's not my responsibility anymore. You'd think a man with kids . . . Well, never mind. He never did call me back, so I went down to the marina to check things out for myself."

"Does Jason live aboard the *Money Honey*?" It was a beautiful boat, but it was a lobster boat and the marina prohibited liveaboards.

"Good heavens, no. He has a place in town. But like Jason owns half this house, I own half the *Money Honey*. I was checking on my investment."

"Was Emmy there?" That's where this tale was going, right? The discovery of Jason and Emmy in flagrante delicto.

"No, but her stuff was. Jason wasn't there, so I went aboard to investigate. In the cabin I found a little carryall with her stuff in it. Intimate stuff. Right out on the bunk for anybody to see."

The "anybody" Pru spoke of would have had to look pretty hard to have found Emmy's undies. Boats like the *Money Honey* were working boats, not cabin cruisers. The area belowdecks on most lobster boats was used for storage with maybe a bunk for the occasional overnight run. The quarters were cramped, uncomfortable, and rarely had windows, so anything inside wouldn't have been visible from the dock. Pru hadn't been inspecting the *Money Honey* for damage. She'd been doing some pretty deep snooping.

"Are you sure the carryall was Emmy's?"

"Who else's would it have been?"

"You said yourself your ex-husband was a dog. You can imagine there might be more than one woman. Emmy told me she couldn't rule it out. And it happened during your marriage."

"They were *hers*." Pru spoke through gritted teeth. "Cheap crap, too."

I doubted Pru was in a position to call Emmy's underthings crap. I would have bet a million dollars that Pru's unmentionables came from Reny's, Maine's deep discount chain. But she did sound absolutely positive about Jason and Emmy.

"What did you do when you found the stuff?" I asked.

"Forbid my kids from going to the marina for one thing. I didn't want to be responsible for whatever they would see if they looked for their dad on his boat. And then, I gave Jason a piece of my mind."

I remembered how on the Saturday of the clambake I'd thought Pru was more aggressive with Jason than usual. I'd had the sense she was scolding him.

"I told him what I told you," Pru continued. "I was not having him divert money to that woman. He told me she was nothing to him. He was ready to end it. That's what I think happened. She thought she was set for life. He broke up with her. Emmy Bailey killed him."

This was too much. According to Emmy, they had hardly *begun* a relationship. "She strangled him with her bare hands and hid him under the woodpile?" I challenged her. It was more than fifty yards from where the police thought Jason was murdered to where his body was found. "If Emmy weighs a hundred and twenty pounds soaking wet I'd be surprised." But didn't that same logic eliminate Pru as the killer?

"That's where Terry Durand comes into it. He has such a weird fixation with her. He'd do anything she asked him to." Pru slapped her hands down on the table, triumphant.

The conversation had started off badly and then veered to terrible. "Did you tell the police this story?" I hoped not.

"I didn't think of it until just now while we were talking. But maybe I will."

Great. This was all Terry needed, an alleged accomplice. All I'd accomplished was to give Pru the idea to accuse him. I turned the conversation to the reason I'd originally come. "Where did Jason's money come from?"

"Lobstering. You know as well as I do it didn't come from the Snowden Family Clambake." She seemed surprised, not by my boldness in asking the question, but by my need to.

"But how all of a sudden, after all these years?"

"Landings have been good these last seasons. And the new boat made a huge difference. Once he had it, it was like he was pulling gold bars out of the sea."

Did Pru truly believe what she was telling me, or had she somehow convinced herself it was true because she loved the newfound family fortune and wanted to keep it coming? Or was she flat-out lying? I couldn't tell. "But where did the money for the boat come from in the first place?" I persisted. "Did your parents buy it?"

She guffawed, a real belly laugh this time. "Who in the world told you that? My mom and dad live on Social Security over in Waldoboro. I send *them* money."

"I heard something about Jason's dad."

"Dead for ten years and worthless when he was alive."

"Then where did the money for the boat come from?" I wasn't going to give up.

"Jason made it lobstering. Hid it from me all those years, even during the divorce. But he made it right in the end."

"Did he have life insurance for the kids?"

"Not that I've heard."

I wasn't surprised. Most lobstermen were fatalists. That's why they didn't learn to swim. But that also meant Pru was worse off with Jason dead. I didn't think that would have escaped her, no matter how angry she was.

"When the cops asked you if Jason had enemies, what did you tell them?"

She pulled another cigarette back out of the pack. She'd worn the previous one down to its component parts. A pile of unburned tobacco, a curl of white paper, and a filter sat on the dining room table. "I told 'em there might be some husbands around town carrying a grudge because my ex-husband had seduced their wives, but I couldn't think why now or why on Morrow Island."

Those were the questions. Why now and why on Morrow Island? It was time to go. She'd given me more time than I deserved. She walked me to the door. "One more thing," I said. "Why didn't you come to work the day Jason died?"

Pru hesitated for a moment. "I might as well tell you. I've told the police. Jason called me. He told me not to go to work. I thought he was sore about the fight with Terry, worried I'd start something with Emmy. The truth is, I was feeling bad about fighting with him. I was happy to have an excuse not to face any of them that day." A tear formed in the corner of her eye. She shook her head, flicking it away. "Now I'll never get to apologize to him."

Her grief wiped away the other stuff—the what and

where of the murder, the question about whodunit—and exposed the core of the tragedy. Jason was dead.

I turned back to her on the porch. "Pru, I really am sorry."

"Honey, I know you are." She closed the door.

Chapter Nineteen

I walked back to Mom's house to pick up the Subaru. Pru was convinced Emmy's relationship with Jason had been much more serious than Emmy had led me to believe. Would Emmy lie to me? She was a friend. But she might if she knew what Jason was mixed up in and thought she was in danger. If she thought her kids were in danger, she would lie her head off. I was convinced of it.

"Hullo, Julia." Emmy seemed surprised to see me at the trailer door. She was dressed in the white button-down shirt and black pants she wore to waitress at Crowley's. "I'm dropping Luther off at Gran's and going to work. Lunch shift at Crowley's."

"That's tough." Lunch at Crowley's on a weekday at the end of the season wouldn't earn her much.

"I know, but I'm lucky. In exchange they gave me nights for the whole long weekend."

Not everyone would think it was lucky to spend three days running her tail off waiting on tables at the clam-bake and then spend her evenings serving the noisy crowd at Crowley's, but Emmy was one determined mom. At least she could have her kids with her on the island. I imagined Vanessa would be sleeping over at Livvie's for the next three nights.

"This won't take long." I stepped inside.

In the tiny living space, a diaper bag was packed for Luther. He sat at the table munching apple pieces, already in a bright red corduroy jacket for the short trip across the lawn to his great-grandmother's.

"I try to feed him before he goes to Gran's to keep things simpler for her. Vanessa can help when she gets home on the school bus." Emmy dug through her bag for her keys. "What did you want?" she asked.

"I've come from Pru's."

Emmy pulled her keys out in triumph. They jangled and Luther reached his arms out, grunting that he wanted them. "How's Pru getting on? She wasn't nice to me, but I do feel sorry for her."

"She's having a hard time of it. So are the kids. How are you doing?"

Emmy bent down and moved the strap of the diaper bag onto her shoulder. "I'm okay. It's weird, you know. To know someone who was murdered, but as I explained, we weren't that close. My life will go on as before, unlike Pru and her kids."

"That's not what Pru says."

Emmy, who was cleaning Luther's face, stopped abruptly. "What do you mean?"

"Pru says you spent a lot of time on the *Money Honey.*"

Emmy dropped the diaper bag on the Formica table with a *thunk*. "I've been on that boat exactly one time, when Jason gave me and the kids a lift home from the clambake. You know Pru was jealous. She reacted all out of proportion to what was truly going on."

"She says you spent enough time on Jason's boat that you left things there. A carryall filled with clothes. Intimate things."

Color flooded into Emmy's face. "That is one hundred percent not true. She's making it up. She's crazy!"

I took a deep breath so I would remain calm. One person flying off the handle in the little space was enough. "Emmy, do you know where Jason's money came from?"

"What do you mean?" The angry flush in her face receded. "He was a highliner. Everybody said so."

"Everybody except the people who would know. The lobstermen at Gus's don't think much of his skills."

She knit her brows. I couldn't tell if she believed me. "I've explained this. Jason and I went on exactly two dates. If you think we discussed our personal finances, you're wrong. I have no idea where his money came from if it wasn't from lobstering."

"Did you ever go to his apartment? Do you know where it is?"

Emmy had lost her patience with me entirely. "I *told* you we had *two* dates. I *never* went to his apartment." She put the diaper bag back on her shoulder and picked Luther up. "Jason lived within walking distance of the marina. That's all I know. I really have to get going."

I walked out with her. She handed Luther to me as she locked the door to the trailer. He put a sticky hand on my chin. I'd distracted Emmy enough she'd washed his face but not his hands. I walked with her over to her gran's house and waited while she reported on the state of Luther's diaper (clean) and his tummy (full). Then we walked to our cars.

"You don't have any idea who the underwear on Jason's boat could belong to." I tried one last time.

Emmy shook her head. "If it's even true. I wouldn't put it past Pru to make the whole thing up."

I thought about trying to find Jason's apartment and maybe even the mystery woman who'd left a bag full of undies on the *Money Honey,* and who had the physical strength to hide Jason's body under the woodpile.

The police would know where the apartment was and would have already searched it. The idea of a female killer seemed far-fetched given the distance the body was moved. The odds were Jason was killed by a man, and that left Dmitri, who had disappeared the day of the murder.

I drove back to town and parked in the municipal lot. Perhaps I could get a read from Binder or Flynn about whether they were looking at Terry or Dmitri.

When I got inside the police station the door to the multipurpose room was shut tight.

"They're-in-a-meeting," Marge the receptionist rat-tat-tatted before I could ask.

"Will you let the lieutenant and the sergeant know I'm looking for them?" I said.

"Sure. When they come out."

Jamie's head poked out from around the partition. "I thought it was you."

I walked back into the bullpen. It was empty except for Jamie. "Where is everyone?"

"Out on patrol or at lunch," he answered. "I was about to leave for Gus's."

Inclining my head toward the multipurpose room, I asked, "What's going on in there?"

"Who knows? They don't tell the local yokels much."

"Binder and Flynn aren't like that."

"The state cops are the least of it."

I remembered the two extra tables set up in the multi-purpose room. "Who's the most of it?"

"Feds, mostly. More arriving every day. It's a regular alphabet soup around here."

"For the murder of a lobsterman who worked at a clambake?" Lots of different agencies coordinating. That was probably why Binder had kept me on hold so long the other day.

"I know. We don't get it either, and it looks like no one is going to enlighten us. Sometimes it feels like they don't care about Jason's murder at all."

Binder and Flynn were dedicated detectives. It didn't add up. "What do they care about?"

"Search me." He looked around the bullpen as if to make sure it was empty, though clearly it was. "Listen, I'm glad you came by," he said. "I heard something this morning I think you should know." He paused. "Pete and the chief were going back and forth about the night Terry robbed Hudson's. Trading stories, you know how it is. I heard something I'd never heard before. The cops here in Busman's, they assumed, in fact they still believe, Jason was with Terry at Hudson's that night."

The air whooshed out of my lungs. "They think Jason was *in* the store?"

"More likely driving the getaway car," Jamie answered. "There were no video cameras at Hudson's eleven years ago. There are none there now, either."

"But there's a big sign on the window behind the cash register that says, THIS LOCATION IS MONITORED, with a line drawing of a camera."

"Fake," Jamie said. "Anyway, the old-timers think Jason was waiting in the car and he got scared when he heard the gunfire and took off, stranding Terry. You see where this is going, right?"

I didn't answer right away while I tried to process this new information. "It gives Terry more motive to hate Jason if he ditched him at Hudson's to face the cops." Howland had said Terry had his hands up when he entered the store and didn't resist arrest. Maybe that was because he was stuck. "Is there any evidence Jason was there?"

"No," Jamie admitted. "Supposition."

"Has anyone told this story to Binder and Flynn?"

"Not that I know of. Like I said, it's speculation based on Jason and Terry being suspected of doing all their crimes together up to that point, and the way the friendship ended when Terry was arrested." He paused. "I've got to get going. Pete's waiting. I thought you'd like to know what the scuttlebutt is. Who knows what really happened?"

Who, indeed? "What was the name of the clerk again?" I asked Jamie as he headed out the door.

"Christopher Gray."

Christopher. The same name as my boyfriend. It hadn't struck me the first time I'd heard it. "You don't know where he is now by any chance?"

"No idea."

Chapter Twenty

I drove to the marina to confront Terry with this new information. Whether Jason had been at Hudson's that night or not, the story was kicking around the Busman's Harbor PD and it wouldn't be long before it made it to Binder and Flynn.

The *Dark Lady* was at her mooring, but Terry was nowhere around. It was weird that he didn't have a cell phone. Or rather, it made perfect sense he didn't have one, but it was weird to be dealing with a person who didn't. I scribbled a note on a Dunkin' Donuts bag I found in my car, left it secured on the *Dark Lady,* and drove back to my apartment.

Downstairs, Gus's was full and loud. The smells made my stomach growl. Upstairs in my apartment, I got out my laptop.

The World Wide Web told me that a Christopher Gray, who was about the right age, lived in Raymond, Maine, about an hour and a half away. Without Terry, my only path forward was to talk to the only other person who'd been in that store.

I drove down Route 1 from our peninsula and flew over the Wiscasset Bridge, empty of summer traffic. Almost to Bath, at the peak of the Sagadahoc Bridge, I looked down at Bath Iron Works and the US Navy ships at their docks being built or refitted.

I had no plan except to find out what had happened. I had Gray's address from the Web, nothing else. He could be at work. He could be away. He could be the wrong Christopher Gray. The trip started to feel desperate. I stayed on Route 1 all the way to Freeport, where I began the trip west.

Route 95 was the major artery in Maine. A super-highway, it took you from the New Hampshire border to Canada, traveling roughly northward with a few zigs and zags to accommodate natural barriers and pass through or near our major cities, Portland, Augusta, and Bangor. Route 1, the scenic route, also took you from New Hampshire to Canada, but along the seacoast. Though your definition of "scenic" might vary. In the more pop-ulated parts of the state it was lined by the same strip malls, service stations, discount centers, snarled traffic, and stoplights found along the rest of US 1.

Traveling east to west in Maine was a different matter. Highways were scarce and most of the routes were two-lane roads through small towns. The seacoast was my Maine, but Maine was a big state, especially by the standards of New England, and it didn't take many miles to feel the sea recede behind me as the lakes and moun-tains came into focus.

I had stumbled into this trip at absolute peak foliage. If the storm the previous week had been a few days later, it would have taken most of the leaves with it, disap-pointing the tourists who came in cars, buses, and cruise ships to see the colors. Last week most of the leaves had been supple enough to cling to their branches. The road was uncrowded and gave me the time to enjoy the bright reds, vibrant yellows, and different shades of orange as I drove.

In an hour and twenty minutes I was in Raymond, Maine, bumping down the side road where Christopher Gray lived. Raymond was a tourist town, like Busman's Harbor, only profoundly different. At the head of Sebago Lake, it was a homing point for people who loved another Maine. Not lighthouses and whale watches, but swimming and boating in fresh water, hiking, camping, air that smelled piney not salty. It was a Maine I loved, but since their season overlapped almost entirely with our own, one I rarely got to visit.

Christopher Gray lived in a small house deep in the woods. A one-door garage was on the ground floor along with a slider that might have led to a finished basement. A set of wooden stairs, stained white, led up one story to a large deck and the front door. There was an old blue hatchback in the driveway and I dared to hope Gray might be at home.

I climbed the stairs. There was no view of the lake, but the woods were peaceful. There were enough leaves down I could catch a glimpse of a yellow house, similar in size and shape, about a hundred yards away through the trees. I pressed the bell.

A woman about my age opened the door and spoke to me through the screen. She was plainly surprised to see me. "Yes?" She kept the screen door between us as I would have done if a stranger turned up on my deck.

"Is Christopher here?"

"He's at work." Her shoulders relaxed a little when

I mentioned Christopher's name, like I wasn't a total stranger, but her guard went up again the moment she realized she'd told me she was likely the only person at home. Or she was the only adult, though I didn't see any toys on the deck or scattered around the yard. "He's on his way home," she said quickly. "I'm his wife. Can I help you?"

"I'm Julia Snowden from Busman's Harbor. Christopher worked there when he was twenty." Both sentences were true. I hoped she would fill in the blank in some meaningful way.

"I'm Rosalind." She smiled but kept the screen between us. "Topher—that's what my husband's called—his grandparents had a house in Busman's Harbor, so he could afford to live there while he worked summer jobs when he was in school. They're both gone now. I never met them. He and I met four years ago. I don't know much about his time there. Except—"

She didn't say it and I mentally filled in the blank. *Except that he was shot.* He would have told her that. "Do you mind if I wait?" I pointed to a pair of Adirondack chairs, stained white like the deck, each with a few dead leaves caught along the joint where the back met the seat. After my drive I would have liked to go in and use the restroom, but I wouldn't have let me had the situation been reversed.

"Suit yourself." So he really was on his way home. She started to swing the wooden door closed, then stopped. "You're not here to announce you've been raising his love child or anything, are you?" She laughed when she said it, but it was a reasonable question in the circumstances.

I rushed to reassure her. "Nothing like that."

She smiled again and closed the door. I brushed the leaves off the nearest chair and sat down to wait. I was sure Rosalind was calling her husband that very minute. It was certainly what I would have done. The afternoon was cool but not cold. A low sun filtered through the colorful leaves.

Topher Gray arrived in fifteen minutes exactly. Rosalind had been right about that. He parked an older Camry behind his wife's car and got out, taking time to retrieve a briefcase and thermos. He wore a short-sleeved shirt untucked over navy pants, the definition of "business casual." I wondered what he did for a living.

He squinted as he came up the stairs, trying to place me. He hadn't recognized my name when Rosalind phoned him, but I bet he thought he would remember me once he saw me. He didn't and I couldn't place him, either. He'd worked at Busman's Harbor several summers, according to Rosalind, so it wasn't impossible I'd seen him. I was in college myself at the time, but I'd worked at the clambake, twelve hours a day, seven days a week. During those summers we'd lived on Morrow Island, so Topher and I wouldn't have had much chance to meet.

I stood and stuck out my hand. "Julia Snowden. Thank you for seeing me." Rosalind could have ordered me away.

He shook my hand. "Christopher Gray, but you know that. Call me Topher. I admit to being curious. We're a long drive from Busman's Harbor. What brings you here?"

There was no point in dancing around it. "I want to talk to you about the night you were shot."

He took a small step backward. He hadn't expected

that. I thought he might tell me to go away. He seemed to weigh the possibilities in his mind. "All right. Let me put my things inside. Do you want something to drink?"

"Water would be great."

He was gone about five minutes. The sun had sunk lower and he flicked on the outside lights with his elbow as he carried two water glasses from the kitchen. Unlike Rosalind, he'd left the door open when he went inside. Evidently he'd decided I was harmless.

"Can I ask, what is your interest in what happened to me?" he said.

There was no point in evading that question, either. "Did you know Terry Durand got out of prison five weeks ago?"

He took a sip of water and nodded. "I knew it was around now."

"How do you feel about that?"

"I don't think you finished answering my question." His tone was neutral, not hostile.

"Terry Durand is my boyfriend's brother. My family runs the Snowden Family Clambake on Morrow Island. There's been a murder there. The police may be looking at Terry for the murder. My boyfriend is convinced his brother isn't involved and Terry denies it. But he has always denied shooting you, too. I want your perspective."

Topher nodded. "I get it. I think. But I'm not sure I can help." He shifted forward in the Adirondack chair, bringing his face closer to mine. "I grew up in Westbrook, Maine. My grandparents had a place in Busman's Harbor. It was nothing to brag about, a two-bedroom cottage in the woods, but I loved it. My favorite memories from being a kid were the weeks my sister and I spent with them in the summer. So when I was in high school, I looked for summer jobs in town. My second year I got lucky—a good job at Lawson's Lumberyard. It didn't offer the kind of money kids got from tips working in the nice restaurants, but it was steady and they gave me plenty of hours. I went back four summers in a row.

"The summer between my sophomore and junior years in college, I decided not to go back to school in the fall. I was going to stay at the cottage after my grandparents left. Since it was only heated by a wood stove, it was kind of nuts, really. I knew they'd cut my hours at Lawson's once the season was over, so I took a second job at Hudson's, six p.m. to closing, five nights a week. I'd be the only one there after eight."

"Were you scared when you were there alone at night?"

"Not really. Sometimes when I'd closed up and turned off the outside lights and had to walk to my car, it was a little creepy, but otherwise, no. I never thought about it. It's Busman's Harbor, right?"

"Right," I agreed.

"I saw Durand come in that night. I'd seen him before. I didn't like the look of him. He went to the back, to the cooler. He was the only customer in the store. I watched him in this convex mirror we had over the checkout counter. He took a six-pack out of the cooler, calm as you please, and stuck it under his jacket."

Topher paused and took another sip of water. I wondered if this was getting too intense, but he gave no sign of it.

"So, like the twenty-year-old great, big idiot I was, I decided to confront him. He started to run and I grabbed his shirt, and next thing I know we're rolling around on the floor. And then *bang*! The loudest noise I've ever heard. I tried to get up but I couldn't."

"You saw him shoot you?"

"Nope. Never saw it. My memory is a little swiss-cheesy around the incident. The way it is in my head, we're fighting and then I'm shot."

"You didn't see him shoot you?"

"I don't *remember* him shooting me."

"But you testified he did in court."

"I did not. The prosecutor never asked me that question. He knew I couldn't remember. He only asked me questions like 'Was I working at Hudson's on the night of . . . etc.?' Most important, he asked me if I could identify Durand as the man I fought with. Which I could."

"As the man you fought with, not as the man who shot you? He was convicted of armed robbery and aggravated assault with a firearm."

"The first cop on the scene testified when he arrived I was bleeding on the floor and Durand was the only other person there, the gun was in the next aisle and so on. That was enough."

"What else do you remember from that night?"

"Like I said, swiss-cheesy. I remember after I was shot Durand had this horrified look on his face. He ran to the housewares aisle and got a bunch of dish towels and tried to stop the bleeding. I was in shock, both by what had happened and physically. I was in and out after that. My ears were ringing. I couldn't hear a thing. I don't remember the paramedics or the ride to the hospital."

"Did you testify to that in court, that he tried to help you?"

"Yes. His attorney asked me what happened after I heard the shot and I told it. Later, the prosecutor told me that it probably made the jury more convinced he did it."

"Why was that?"

"Because he showed remorse. The jury put themselves in his position. They would have been horrified if they'd done it. But Durand did shoot me during the commission of an armed robbery, so they convicted him."

"Did you know Terry Durand has always claimed he was innocent? Didn't plead guilty, wouldn't admit guilt to get parole?" I asked.

"I did. But someone shot me, and there was no one else in that store."

"Did you see anyone else that night?"

"Durand was the only one I saw in the store."

"What about out by the gas pumps? Was there anyone in a car, anyone you would recognize?"

"No. Sorry. I always told the cops, Durand was the only one I saw. The only one I could remember." We sat in silence for a moment after that. "I'm sorry I couldn't be more help," he finally said.

I stood and he did, too. "Don't apologize." I shook his hand. "It was good of you to see me at all. What happened after you were shot?"

"I was lucky. He hit me in the shoulder. Missed the bone. I went back to school that winter semester. I was done with taking time off."

"Do you still think about it? Often, I mean."

He shrugged. He seemed to have full movement in his shoulder. "Not so much anymore. It's been ten years."

The screen door slammed and Rosalind was on the

deck. She was heavily pregnant, something I hadn't been able to see when we talked through the screen door. "He has nightmares," she said. She must have listened to the whole conversation. "Not often, but he does, and they are terrible. He wakes up screaming."

He put his arms around her. "I'm okay," he said. "We're okay."

I thanked them both and returned to the Subaru.

Chapter Twenty-One

It was after seven and almost fully dark by the time I hit the main road heading east. The few cars coming toward me lowered their brights as they passed. The rest of the time it was the Subaru's headlights on the road and a line of ghostly trees on either side, like driving through a tunnel.

There wasn't a big dinner at Mom's house planned for that evening and I was grateful. Mom, Marguerite, and Tallulah were taking a night off, eating leftover pot roast. The magnet that had drawn us, Lilly Smythe's journal, was done. It had left Lilly perched on a rock overlooking the channel between Morrow Island and Westclaw Point, contemplating ending her life. Had she gone through with it? I felt for her, so scared and alone. I longed to reach out to her across the century and tell her it wasn't her fault, she had nothing to be ashamed of.

I drove on, shoulders tense, hands clenched on the steering wheel. The cozy, domestic scene at the Gray's house had made me . . . angry. The fact that he shared a name with my boyfriend seemed to mock me. Topher and Rosalind were my age and they had a house and a baby on the way. I was in love with a man whose genes might hold a horrific disease, whose brother might return to prison, who was estranged from the rest of his family. Why couldn't I have a white picket fence and a couple of kids like all those women who had gathered in Pru's living room? Why did life have to be so complicated? It seemed like a modest desire, to be like the Grays, a small house, a small family.

I'd driven all afternoon, and for what? Out of some desperate need to keep moving, because I couldn't think of what else to do. Chris sometimes observed that I'd failed to leave my New York City pace behind. Maybe he was right. Maybe I was a workaholic nutcase.

Chris had asked me to help his brother. So far I had discovered that Jason might have left Terry high and dry at Hudson's, driving off and leaving him stranded to face a felony charge. That was a good reason for a long-simmering hatred of Jason Caraway. I'd mentally eliminated Emmy and Pru as suspects. Not motivated enough and not physically strong enough. The same probably went for the mystery woman who belonged to the bag of undies aboard the *Money Honey*.

That left Dmitri. He was the suspect left standing. I had to find out where he'd gone and why. But how? He was the best hope to offer the cops a focus besides Terry.

The road went on and I was back in familiar territory. I started to feel badly as I drove up Route 1. Who was I to think my life was uniquely challenging? Those women at Pru's house weren't any different from me. Pru had endured a cheating husband. She worked two hard jobs to provide for her family. Livvie had had a miscarriage and had waited and hoped for five years after it for her second pregnancy. She was married to Sonny, and though I loved my brother-in-law, that was more than enough. Even Topher and Rosalind, whom I'd seen as the perfect couple, had their own issues. Topher had been shot, for goodness sake. He woke up screaming in the night.

My life wasn't worse than anyone else's. I was luckier than most. I physically shook myself. "Stop feeling sorry for yourself, Julia."

When I was on the highway that led down our peninsula from Route 1, I called Chris and asked him to pick up Terry at the marina and bring him to our apartment.

Terry and Chris were in the apartment when I got home. I'd parked at Mom's and walked to Gus's. The day had turned chilly when the sun went down, chillier than I was dressed for. I hugged myself as I came up the stairs.

Both men stood up from the couch to greet me. They were subdued and it was obvious this was no time for chitchat.

"What's going on?" Terry asked. "Why am I here?"

Now that I was home, I wasn't in a hurry to have this conversation. I felt badly for Terry, I really did. In Chris's telling Terry had difficult growing up years, never really accepted, picked on and worse by Chris's dad, Terry's stepfather. And, like Chris, there was a 50 percent chance he'd inherited his mother's Huntington's disease. The man had spent ten years in prison. He was broke and jobless.

"A friend of mine on the Busman's PD told me the cops think Jason was with you that night at Hudson's," I said.

Terry sighed and looked down at his hands. "I never told them that."

"Was Jason there?" I asked. "You can't hurt him by telling me."

"That's true," Terry said. "But I can hurt myself. The cops are working up to Jason's murder being some old beef between him and me. I can feel it. When I was in for my second interview, they asked more about me and Jason than they did about what I did the morning he was killed. Which was weird because as you know, I have next to no alibi."

"You're worried if you tell me what happened that night at Hudson's, the DA can call me to testify you had your reasons to hate Jason," I said. "But isn't that hearsay?"

Terry looked at the floorboards, worrying his hands. "I'm not a lawyer and I don't play one on TV. There were guys on the inside who spent all day and night studying the law and reviewing their cases, even filing appeals. I never thought it was worth it. 'Keep moving forward' was my motto. Do the time. Never look back."

"I'm asking you to look back now," I said. "Was Jason at the store that night? Was he the getaway driver? I went to visit the man you shot today."

"Christopher Gray," Terry said. "Did he see Jason at Hudson's that night?"

"No," I answered.

"I knew he didn't." Terry was quiet for so long I assumed he wasn't going to answer. I was forming a plea in my head, hoping to move him, when he started to talk. "You know, I never pled guilty to shooting that clerk. Never said I did it, in court or anywhere else. I never said it in a parole hearing. That's why I did my full time."

"We know," Chris said.

"That's because I didn't shoot him. I didn't even bring a gun."

Chris and I both stared at him.

"How were you going to hold up Hudson's without a gun?" Chris was irritated. Terry's denials always irritated him. He thought his brother was evading responsibility.

"I wasn't. It wasn't an armed robbery. I was shoplifting."

"Shoplifting!" Chris's face betrayed his disbelief. "Why were you shoplifting?"

"Because I was an idiot. And I was high. But that's no excuse. I was long past old enough to know better. Jason and I had done a bunch of stupid stuff. Breaking in to summer homes mostly. No one was ever there. It was dumb, but there was no chance of hurting anybody."

"So if you didn't bring a gun—"

"I went into Hudson's to steal a six-pack. It was stupid. I could have paid for it. I had a job in the kitchen at Schooner Bill's. It didn't pay much but I didn't need much. It was just me.

"Jason was in the car with the motor running. We were going to Fisherman's Park to drink. It was dark. After ten. My plan was simple. I grabbed a six-pack and ran. Except this kid in the store, he thought he was a hero. He spotted me and he ran, too. Tackled me by the cash register at the front of the store on my way out. I don't know, but I figure Jason saw it through the window. Saw him jump and me go down and thought I was in real trouble. I wasn't. The kid had a hold of me, but had no way to call the cops unless he let me go. We were wriggling around on the floor when I heard the gun go off and then the kid screaming bloody murder. I stood up and saw Jason peel out of the parking lot.

"I made sure the kid wasn't so badly hurt. By that time I could hear the sirens. A gunshot attracts a lot of attention that time of night. Like ten neighbors of the store had called the cops. I put my hands up when Pete Howland walked into the store. He was a rookie and my main concern was he didn't shoot me."

"Jason shot the clerk."

"Yup. Jason shot him. I recognized the gun as soon as Howland found it. We'd picked it up in one of the house breaks."

"But the clerk—"

"Testified he saw only me."

"But it must have been obvious he wasn't shot at such close range."

"Do you think the DA was going to use the state's money to pay for ballistics tests and medical testimony in an armed robbery where there's an eyewitness and the perpetrator is standing there with his hands up when the cops walk in? I certainly didn't have money to pay for private tests or experts. My public defender brought me deal after deal, but they all involved me admitting I was guilty, so I said no thanks."

"Why didn't you give Jason up?" Chris asked.

"Because if we were in it together, they'd say I was guilty anyway. Conspiracy to commit a felony. Same sentence as if I shot him. Even I know that. It wouldn't help me, so why drag Jason down? He had a wife and two little kids at home."

"After that, what happened to you and Jason?" I asked him.

"I didn't expect him to attend my trial. Seeing his face might have jogged the kid's memory. Or even to visit me in the county jail. But I thought maybe once I was settled up in Warren, once the trial was over and it was clear Jason wasn't involved, I thought maybe he would visit me then."

"Were you angry that he didn't?"

Terry's head shot up, but he still didn't look at us. "Are you trying to help me, Julia, or are you trying to get me convicted again?"

"I'm trying to understand your relationship with Jason," I told him. "And I'm not the only one."

"Like I told you, I didn't look back then, and I don't like looking back now. I wouldn't have killed Jason for something that happened in the past."

"Would you have killed him for something that happened in the present?" I asked.

"You mean Emmy. I told you, no. I never in my life ever wanted to kill anyone, and that includes when I was in the army and it was my job."

Terry moved toward the stairs. "Look, both of you, I appreciate what you've tried to do for me. I really do. But let's face facts. I'm the only person close to Jason's murder who's been convicted of shooting someone. Whatever is going to happen is going to happen."

"It's not as grim as you think," I said. "There's still the missing demolition guy. If Binder and Flynn thought they had a case against you, you'd have been arrested by now."

Terry fixed his eyes on mine. "Promise me one thing, Julia. When it's time to run, you'll tell me."

Chapter Twenty-Two

I slept poorly, Terry's request sounding in my ears. Would I tell him when it was time to run? No, I would not. If Binder and Flynn had enough to arrest him, I'd let justice take its course.

Would I tell Chris, which might be tantamount to telling Terry? That was a harder one. Chris's and my relationship had been one of peeling away secrets, getting to greater levels of intimacy. We were in a good place now, and if I found out Terry was about to be arrested I wouldn't keep it from Chris. He had hated Terry's crime—or what he'd believed his crime to be. I could trust Chris to do the right thing, whatever it was.

It took a long time to work it all out, and I woke up feeling tired and down.

In the morning I had an appointment to meet Floradale Thayer at Mom's garage so she could decide if there were any of Lilly Smythe's belongings she wanted to take for the Busman's Harbor Historical Society. Tallulah had volunteered to help, so I went into Mom's house to get her.

"How did you do on the Web?" I asked her.

"You were right," Tallulah answered. "I couldn't find a Lilly Smythe anywhere in Maine or Massachusetts after 1898. I can't bear the idea that she killed herself."

"You wouldn't find her by that name if she married," I pointed out. "You don't know what happened."

Tallulah shivered, the only indication I'd ever seen that she was cold, though I doubted that was why she did. "But the sealed room. I think it means something terrible happened. It must have."

We went out to the unused third bay in Mom's garage where the belongings moved from Lilly's room were stored. I'd told family members to take something as a remembrance and most of them had. After all these decades we felt someone should honor the poor young woman who had been so terrified and alone. I had selected her wire-framed spectacles. They were personal and a reminder of her vulnerability.

Tallulah helped me open the double doors to that part of the garage. The sun shone onto the pile of objects. It didn't look like much, the plain bureau, writing desk, nightstand, disassembled bed frame, rolled up mattress, and three plastic crates. Back in Lilly's room in their original places, the pieces looked like they belonged in a museum. Piled like any other family's cheap hand-me-downs, the stuff seemed destined for a booth at the Busman's Harbor Stop 'n' Swap. I doubted the historical society would have an interest.

"We should have brought Mrs. Thayer out to the island," I muttered. "I would have if there hadn't been a murder."

"What?" Tallulah asked.

"Nothing. Talking to myself."

A metallic cough came from the driveway and Floradale Thayer's old blue van sputtered into view.

The springs groaned as Floradale alighted. I glanced at Tallulah, hoping she wouldn't stare, but of course she did.

Floradale Thayer was enormous, well over six and a half feet tall with the shoulders of a linebacker. She wore a khaki skirt and olive green sweater that stretched across her broad chest. In her midsixties, she walked in a ramrod-straight posture that might have come from the military, but instead came from Miss Lyon's Ballroom Dancing School for Young Ladies and Gentlemen.

We greeted each other and I introduced Tallulah as my cousin.

"Cousin you say?" Mrs. Thayer knew the genealogy of every family in town, with special emphasis on the prominent summer families like the Morrows. "You're one of the Boston family," she said to Tallulah, who nodded. The story of how I'd discovered two branches of my mother's family tree she never knew existed was well known around town and especially by Mrs. Thayer, who had helped me with my early research.

"What have you got here?" She looked into the garage.

"We found this at Windsholme," I answered.

"In a sealed-off room," she said. We had already covered this ground on the phone. "Most interesting."

She dismissed the desk, bureau, nightstand, and iron bedstead out of hand. "There's one of these in half the cottages on the peninsula." Only a slight exaggeration. "But let's see some of the personal effects."

I opened the first of the plastic bins, which contained most of Lilly's clothes. Mrs. Thayer pulled them out one at a time, unfolding them. "Marvelous," she said, holding the bathing costume in front of her. She handed it off to Tallulah, who played along, holding out her arms to receive them like a salesperson in a high-end boutique.

By then Mrs. Thayer was on to Lilly's skirt and blouse. "Fantastic," she said. "Likely a governess. Late eighteen-nineties." She knew her stuff. "I'll take all the clothes."

When she pulled out a nightgown a shiver ran down my spine. It had a whole new meaning now that I knew about the awful entry in Lilly's journal.

"Have you ever heard of a governess at Windsholme in 1898 called Lilly Smythe?" I asked Floradale. If word of Lilly's suicide had gotten around town it wasn't out of the question Mrs. Thayer would have known about it.

"Can't say as I have," she replied.

"It's spelled S-M-Y-T-H-E," Tallulah said helpfully.

"Is she local?" Mrs. Thayer was barely paying attention. She was bent over the second container, the one filled with the books and personal items.

"We think she came from Boston," I said. At least that was where she'd met the Morrow yacht.

"No, sorry." Mrs. Thayer shook her head. "What happened to her?"

"That's what we're trying to find out," Tallulah answered. Then she and I, alternating and filling in details, told the story we had found in the journal.

Mrs. Thayer furrowed her brow. Mysteries from the past were her bread and butter. Every day during every season people turned up at the historical society having traced their origins to a grave in the Busman's Harbor cemetery where the trail ran cold. She helped everyone she could.

"I can tell you what happened to Frederick Morrow," she said at last. "He drowned. During a boat race at the yacht club. He was drunk and fell out. Even though there were many witnesses, he was out of sight by the time the sailboat came about and returned to the spot. His body washed up in the marina ten days later."

"Seems like rough justice," Tallulah muttered, an icy cold assessment given her sunny disposition, though accurate, I thought.

"Did this governess mention any surnames of the other servants that summer?" Mrs. Thayer asked. "Because if they were local, there may still be family around. They may have heard stories. It's a long shot, but what have you got to lose?"

I thought back through the stories, but Tallulah, who'd read each entry at least twice, beat me to the punch. "The cook was Mrs. Stout and the housekeeper Mrs. Franklin."

Mrs. Thayer shook her head. "Not familiar."

"Mrs. Stout worked for William Morrow in New York City. My grandmother remembers her. Mrs. Franklin wasn't a good housekeeper according to the journal. I doubt she lasted long." Tallulah paused, scrunching up her face. "There were maids who came from Busman's Harbor, but I don't think even their first names are mentioned in the journal."

"Well, it was worth a thought," Mrs. Thayer said.

"Wait!" Tallulah's eyes lit up. "There was also the captain of the Morrow yacht. He was a former naval officer. His name was Beal, I think. Captain Beal."

"Well, that's different," Mrs. Thayer replied. "There's Beals all over the place around here. If I were you, I would start my inquiries with Bill Beal. He's the family history buff. Stops in the society all the time. I'll call you with his contact information when I get back to the office."

"Thank you!" Tallulah was excited. I worried she had her hopes too high. A family legend about the suicide of a governess who'd spent less than three months on an island in Maine a hundred and twenty years ago? It seemed far-fetched there would be family stories anyone would remember. But any clue was better than none. That was certainly the way Tallulah viewed it.

Mrs. Thayer repacked the books. Tallulah refolded the clothes and prepared to return them to the other container. "Wait, there's one more thing in the bottom of this bin you haven't seen." Tallulah lifted a pair of bloomers out of the container. They were still folded with the same sharp creases they'd had in the drawer. Since they were the third identical pair, we'd never unfolded them. As they unfurled something fell out, splat onto the driveway.

Tallulah and I spotted it at the same moment. "Another volume of the journal!" She pounced, picking it up. The notebook was identical to the one we'd read from every evening the past week.

Floradale Thayer eyed the cover. "Would you want to donate that to the historical society? We'd be happy to take it, along with the other. They would be a valuable reference about life in a Maine summer residence."

"Not now." Tallulah clutched the journal close.

"Maybe someday," I added.

Tallulah and I helped Floradale load the three plastic bins into her wheezy old van. Then we went into Mom's kitchen to clean up and get something to drink. Marguerite and Mom were at the kitchen table with cups of coffee in front of them.

"We found another volume of Lilly's journal, Granny!" Tallulah practically danced. Marguerite put out her hand. Tallulah gave her the notebook and then went to the kitchen sink to wash off the dust. I filled Mom in on what Floradale had taken from the garage while Marguerite turned the pages of the new volume.

"We'll donate the bed and the other furniture," Mom said, "if no one in the family can use them."

"And take the mattress to the dump," I added.

"This book is blank." Marguerite sounded bitterly disappointed. "There's nothing in it. This must have been an extra notebook Lilly brought with her for the summer but never used."

Tallulah poured a cup of coffee and joined them at the table. "I was so hoping we'd get answers."

While I took my turn at the sink, my phone rang. I stepped into the hall to answer it. It was Floradale Thayer with Bill Beal's contact information as promised. I returned to the kitchen and told the others about it.

"Bill Beal from the East Busman's General Store?" Mom asked.

"Yes. Mrs. Thayer said the phone number at the store was the best way to reach him," I answered.

"Marvelous. We should all visit him there," Mom said.

East Busman's was a charming village a few miles out of town. At its center, homes and shops faced a lovely green with a large millpond. There were two antiques shops, a small gallery, and a fancy restaurant.

The general store was the heart of the village. It was the best parts of a supermarket, convenience store, hardware store, and boat shop, with a post office window that would sell you stamps or mail your packages. It was the place to go if you lived on the east side of our peninsula and didn't want the bother of going into town to get your errands done, especially during the summer when parking was at a premium. It was also rightfully renowned for its pizza, which was the best in the area, and its ice cream, which came from a dairy on the next peninsula.

"We'll have lunch there," Mom said. "And if he's in, we'll pick Bill Beal's brain for any family stories. We'll bring the journal. Julia, do you want to come?"

I was about to say yes when Marguerite spoke. "There is writing in the back of this notebook, but it's not Lilly Smythe's."

That stopped us all.

"Look." Marguerite held a page out for us to inspect.

"Is that some kind of code?" Tallulah asked.

Marguerite shook her head. "No. It's Cyrillic, the alphabet used in Russian and related languages."

"Do you read Russian?" I asked. Was there no end to how amazing this woman was?

Marguerite laughed. "No. I recognize the script is all. And it's modern. These passages were written with a ballpoint pen."

"Can I see it?"

Marguerite handed me the notebook. There were five pages of writing in blue ballpoint pen. Toward the end of the text, the letters lightened and then petered out, like the pen had run out of ink. Whoever had written it had pressed down hard, leaving impressions of the letters on the blank pages all the way to the back of the notebook. Because the letters were from an alphabet different from my own, I couldn't tell whether the handwriting was masculine or feminine.

My heart began to beat wildly. The notebook had been left in the sealed-off room. It was modern, written with a ballpoint pen, so that meant it had been left there sometime after the demo crew had opened the wall. Dmitri had been in that room. Perhaps he had left the note to indicate where he had gone or what had happened.

Fortunately, I knew someone who could translate it for me.

"I'm going to take this," I told them. "The three of you work on the Beal angle." I put the notebook into my tote bag.

"Suit yourself," Mom said. "Wherever you're headed, our assignment is going to be more fun."

Chapter Twenty-Three

I didn't wait for the others to organize themselves to leave. I headed straight down to the town pier and got in our Boston Whaler. The demo crew was back on Morrow Island and Alex would be with them. He would tell me what the pages in the Cyrillic script said.

As I approached the island, I was both sorry and relieved to see the solitary seal still hauled out on his rocky perch at the end of the island. "Hey, boy," I called as I went past. "It's time to leave here, just like the humans."

The police tape still fluttered around the woodpile. Since the island had been cleared for use, I took it down, wrapping the yellow plastic around my left hand. It wouldn't do to have the tourists see it on Saturday. I threw it in a covered trash can on my way past the dining pavilion.

At Windsholme, the *whump* of the sledgehammers, the whine of electric saws, and the crash of debris thrown into the dumpster signaled the demo crew was hard at work. I walked through the slowly disappearing rooms and found Joe, the crew boss, and two others in the nursery. Alex wasn't with them and I assumed he was in another part of the house working with the other guy. When I looked in Lilly's room, sure enough, there was a second doorway in the framing leading to Frederick Morrow's bedroom, visible now that the plaster was gone.

"You want something, missus?" Joe asked.

"No. Just looking." I smiled politely at the crew like an owner who'd come to check on progress, then I headed back down the hall to the back stairs, looking in each room for Alex. I didn't find him.

I sat on the steps to the front porch to wait. While the men could send the debris down a chute they'd attached to a window on the second floor, they would have to use the stairs and come across the porch to use the restroom. The public bathrooms at the Snowden Family Clambake were down on the great lawn behind the dining pavilion. Sooner or later, each member of the crew would have to walk by me. Meanwhile, the porch roof would shelter me from prying eyes on the second and third floors.

It wasn't a flawless plan. Three men came in and out while I waited, each one eyeing me as he passed. Soon Joe arrived, alerted no doubt by one of the others. "Do you need something, missus?" he asked.

"No. I'm enjoying the day," I answered, which was lame, but appeared to work. He shrugged and moved on.

Finally, Alex came out the front door, and thank goodness he was alone.

"I need to speak to you." I kept my voice low. "I'll meet you in the dining pavilion in ten minutes."

He walked across the lawn toward the bathrooms. I waited a good five minutes and then went to the pavilion, settling at a picnic table in the October sunshine.

Alex entered the dining room, looking for me. "Over here!" I called. He glanced both ways over his shoulder as if he might have been followed.

"What are you doing here?" He was clearly upset.

"I need to talk to you. I didn't know how to reach you."

"Have the police found Dmitri?" He sounded so hopeful, I hated to tell him no.

"Nothing like that. You haven't heard anything?"

"No one says a word. It is like he was never here."

"Sit down. Just for a few minutes. I have something I want you to look at." He sat across from me and I pulled the second notebook out of my tote bag and opened it to the first page of the Cyrillic script. "I need you to translate this."

He frowned. "Where did you get this?"

"From here, in the house. It was hidden among the clothes in the bureau in the sealed-off room. What does it say?"

He studied the page. As he did, the color drained from his face and his Adam's apple quivered. "This isn't Russian."

"Oh." I was deeply disappointed. I'd been sure Dmitri was going to tell us where he was.

"It's Ukrainian. But I can read it. The two languages are very similar." He was silent as he turned the pages, moving his lips occasionally as he read. At last, he closed the volume.

"What does it say?" I asked.

"I will not tell you."

"What? Are you kidding?" My voice was louder than I intended.

Alex looked over his shoulder. "Shush!"

"You need to tell me what this says."

"No. It is too dangerous for you to know. It is too dangerous for me to know. You must burn this."

"Don't be ridiculous. I'm not going to burn it."

"Get rid of it when you get to the mainland. Forget you ever had it. It is dangerous to you, and since I have read it, it is dangerous to me. I will tell no one. You mustn't either." Alex was plainly terrified.

"Alex." I spoke with the voice I used when I caught our young employees doing something stupid or dangerous. "Tell me what it says."

His shoulders slumped. "Okay. But then you must get rid of it." He swallowed and began. "This was written by a young woman, a Ukrainian. She does not say her name." He paused, swallowing hard again.

I got up from the picnic table and retrieved some water from the cooler on the other side of the room. When I gave it to him, he downed it in one gulp.

"What was this woman's notebook doing inside Windsholme?" I asked him.

Alex closed the notebook. "You know there are people who bring others across the border internationally, right? People without proper papers?"

I sat back down across from him. "Yes."

"This young woman was brought into the United States from Canada. She was left on your island during the storm last week. She was scared and hungry. She found the little room. She stayed there very afraid."

"But why was she on the island?"

Finally, he spoke. "This is what I have suspected.

What I have feared. They think they don't talk about it in front of me because I am young, but we are always together. I have heard many things." He let out a long breath before he continued the story of what he had read. "The woman was supposed to be dropped at a harbor farther south, where she could easily get on a bus or train. Because of the storm, she was left here."

"Was it Dmitri who left her here?" I still wanted to make the Dmitri connection.

He shook his head slowly. "No. She was left here by your friend Jason, the one who was killed."

Jason. Of course it was Jason. Jason who disappeared for days at a time. Jason with all the unexplained money. Jason with the big, fancy boat. The boat Mark Cochran had found for the demo crew wouldn't have made it to the next peninsula.

"Did *she* kill Jason?"

"I don't think so," Alex answered. "It is not in the book, but I think she was gone off the island before he died."

Now I was as frightened as he was. I thought my heart would hammer itself out of my chest. "Did Joe kill Jason because of this human smuggling? Or did Dmitri kill Jason? Is that why he left?"

"I don't know," Alex said. "Whatever happened, I was not here. The day you found your friend's body the rest of them, including Dmitri, came over to the island very early in the morning without me. Oleg and Yuri returned around seven-thirty to pick me up. That is all I know."

"You told me Dmitri had cleared out by the time you got up that morning."

"That is what Joe told me to say."

"You can't go back to work." I had a terrible feeling something would happen to him. "You and I have to leave right now. We'll take the notebook to the police. You have to tell them everything you've told me."

"No."

"If you don't, you'll get arrested and probably deported."

"If I do, Joe will have me killed."

"Alex!" Joe's voice boomed across the open dining room. He spoke rapidly in Russian, judging by the inflection, an alternating stream of rebukes and demands. Alex, whose back was to Joe, leaned across the notebook on the picnic table and then slipped it down into his lap.

"I was just giving him a glass of water." I tried to keep my voice even. Alex still faced me, which was good because if he'd turned around, Joe would have seen the terror in his eyes.

"Water is at the work site." Joe dismissed me, curtly. Then he said, still in English, "Alex, your partner waits for you to do that big part of the job. You slow up everything. Apologize to Mrs. Snowden and get back to work."

"I'm sorry, Mrs. Snowden," Alex said. He handed me his empty cup with his right hand. Under the table he slipped the notebook onto my lap with his left. He didn't want me to have it, but he couldn't be caught with it. Giving it to me was his least bad option. The handoff completed, he got up from the bench, turned around slowly and, head down, shoulders dropping, followed Joe out of the pavilion.

* * *

I had to get out of there, off the island and to the police. I put the journal back in my tote bag and walked to the edge of the pavilion.

Two members of the demo crew were down on the dock. They pretended to do something with their boat, but I wasn't convinced. Joe had sent them to do what? Make sure I left, or prevent me from leaving? I couldn't take the chance. When they were both examining the outboard motor, playing their parts, I took off across the great lawn and into the woods.

I knew the woods better than they did. Enough leaves were off the birches and maples that grew among the evergreens that I could see where I was going. I stopped every ten yards or so to listen for footsteps behind me. The woods were silent. There was only a distant clatter caused by the remaining members of the demo crew inside Windsholme.

I kept moving over the backside of the island toward the little beach. At the point where I rejoined the path, it split, leading down to the cove or up to the boulder that hung over it. I rested. My breathing quieted and I listened. Nothing. I needed to get centered. Panic would get me killed, I was convinced.

The channel between Morrow Island and the mainland was narrow, only about three hundred yards. Lobster buoys painted in bright primary stripes bobbed in the water. Straight across the channel, Quentin Tupper's sleek marble and glass tower stood, rising out of the rocks. Wyatt was probably working there. Pity I had no way to reach her.

I walked to the edge of the boulder, something we'd dared each other to do when we were kids. The end was about thirty feet up and hung over the water, but barely.

Because the little beach was in a protected cove, the shore fell off gradually, giving way to a mucky, rocky bottom. My parents worried about clambake visitors misjudging the depth of the water below and jumping off the boulder, particularly at high tide because it was hard to judge. There was a wooden sign at the end of the path from the woods that warned: DANGER. NO DIVING OR JUMPING. SHALLOW WATER.

If Lilly Smythe had jumped from here and succeeded in her suicide attempt, she had most likely died from a broken neck or back. She wouldn't have drowned. Perhaps a slip from a high place would be easier for her family to accept. I was overwhelmed by the thought of Lilly Smythe plunging to her death. And now this new young woman, the Ukrainian. Had Jason moved her off the island before he was killed? Had the Russians? Where was she?

I considered whether I could swim for it. The air was still, the channel calm and clear, not a ripple on the surface. It wasn't impossible. People did it. But not in October. The water was cooling rapidly. I'd risk hypothermia in addition to the current. No one knew I was attempting it. No one would know where to look for me. It was too risky.

I had two choices. I could go to the little house, get on the radio, and beg someone to call the authorities. Then I would have to wait at least twenty-five minutes, possibly cornered in the house, until they arrived. Or, I could get to the Whaler, go to the mainland and find Binder and Flynn, give them the journal, and tell them what I knew.

I stared into the water, working up my courage. The rocks and branches that had fallen into the water long ago created sepia designs on the mucky bottom. I often studied them, the way people look for patterns or pictures in clouds. But the boulder wasn't working its magic. My fear for Alex's safety and my own kept pushing its way in.

I was about to turn away when I spotted it. At first I thought it was a couple of large rocks forming the head and torso of a man with branches and old marine rope forming the hips and legs. But the more I looked at it, the more I was certain it was a man.

I couldn't be absolutely sure, but there was a man missing from this island and the image of a man was on the bottom, tied up in ropes, perhaps weighted down. My heart raced and I felt bile rise to my throat.

I didn't take the time to be certain. Instead I headed for the dock, moving not over the top of the island past Windsholme and the open lawn, but around through the woods. At times I was able to run, but at others the terrain was too difficult and I had to take my time, thrashing through the underbrush.

I emerged near the woodpile. The dock was deserted. The two Russians must have given up or gone to report to Joe.

I sprinted onto the dock as quickly as I could. There was a shout from up at Windsholme. I looked in time to see the two Russians who'd been on the dock take off running toward me.

Focus, focus, focus. My hands shook as I untied the Whaler and started her up. She was by far the faster boat. If I could get away from the dock they wouldn't be able to catch me. I heard their heavy boots pelting down the wooden planks as the Whaler moved away from the dock. I put the throttle down and sped away as fast as I dared.

When I looked back, the two Russians were on the dock, joined by Joe. They knew they couldn't catch me, but I doubted they would stay there long.

Chapter Twenty-Four

The door to the multipurpose room was closed when I got to the police station.

"I need to see Lieutenant Binder immediately," I told Marge.

"He's in a meeting. I'll let him know you're here when he's done." She stared at me and I realized how I must look—scratched, leaves caught in my clothes, my hair windblown and crazy.

I couldn't wait. I turned the knob and burst through the door.

"You can't go in there!" Marge's voice echoed after me.

Inside, at least two dozen law enforcement personnel stood listening to a man who was at the whiteboard. There were men and women in uniforms, in suits, in shirtsleeves, and in windbreakers, the alphabet soup Jamie had described.

I searched the crowd and found Lieutenant Binder, staring at me like the others. The man at the whiteboard stopped talking.

"I found another body on Morrow Island," I shouted.

"Not on the island. In the channel. And I believe there's a man in danger out there."

Binder stepped forward, put a hand on my shoulder, and looked directly at me. "One thing at a time. Tell us about the body."

As I told them about the body in the water, I blushed furiously. What if I was mistaken and it really was a pile of branches and debris? "I can go with you and show you," I said.

"Why were you on the island?" Binder asked. "You're not open for business today."

I told them about the journal and the Russians and what Alex had told me. The room was silent. Everyone was listening to me. "This man, Alex, who's been helping me, is in danger," I said. "You have to go out there and save him."

"We will," Binder said. "Just a couple more questions."

A man I didn't recognize put on gloves and came to take the journal from me. He lifted the notebook out of my tote and put it in a plastic bag.

"You handled it." Binder nodded toward the journal.

"I did. Alex did. My cousin Tallulah and my cousin Marguerite did. And maybe my mom. And maybe Floradale Thayer. I can't remember."

"We'll talk about this later. The Russians were on the island when you left," Binder confirmed.

"Yes, though that was"—I glanced at the clock on the wall—"thirty minutes ago."

A woman was in the corner of the room, talking on the phone in a low voice, no doubt coordinating with the Marine Patrol, the harbormaster, and the Coast Guard.

"Please wait out in the reception area," Binder directed. "Call Chris. Tell him you're here and you're fine. Don't give him any details. Tell him you'll call him when he can pick you up." As I left, I saw the man who had been at the whiteboard step to the middle of the room.

Minutes later they charged out of the multipurpose room. Through the glass front door of the station house, I watched as some of them ran for the town pier. Others headed in the direction of Bayview Street. A few stayed at the station to coordinate, but no one I knew. I sat on the hard wooden bench across from Marge and waited.

It was almost dark when the part of the group that had gone out to the island returned. They went into the multipurpose room and closed the door. Most of the agents who'd gone to Bayview Street had been back for a while, but no one would tell me anything. Finally, Flynn called me inside.

He introduced me to the man who had been at the whiteboard, Special Agent-in-Charge Winton. The man sat, hands folded on the hard plastic top of the table. Lieutenant Binder was in the chair next to him. "Please join us, Ms. Snowden," Agent Winton said. I sat across from him. Flynn sat next to me.

"Thank you for your help today," Winton started.

"Was there a body in the channel?" They'd been gone so long there must have been. "Was it Dmitri?"

"It was Special Agent Daniel Petrov, working under-cover as Dmitri Mikhailov. He had infiltrated the demo crew because we had credible information they were human smugglers."

I could barely process what they were telling me. "I'm sorry," I said.

"Thank you, for your condolences and for spotting his body and reporting it today. He could have been there much longer if not for your eagle eyes." Winton sounded sincere.

"It was low tide when I was there. I got lucky. I wasn't looking."

"Understood, but you brought your suspicions to us," he said. "You also brought the journal to us. We have a Ukrainian speaker available to the team and we've already had it translated."

I waited, hoping he would tell me how the journal had been important.

Eventually, he did. "We have been on the trail of the Russian you know as Joe for a long time. He's a naturalized US citizen who appears to run a legitimate business doing challenging demolition jobs all over New England. However he also has a side business smuggling people into the United States."

"Human trafficking," I said.

"There is no doubt that some of the people Joe has brought in are ensnared in the sex trade or placed in forms of servitude that amount to slavery. Others like the young woman who wrote in the journal are simply desperate to get into the United States for their own reasons."

"What were hers?"

"Here's what we know about her." He opened his hands and laid them flat on the table. "Her name is Sofiya Makarenko. She is Ukrainian. During the civil war in Ukraine her family was endangered and applied to come to the west as refugees. Sofiya's mother suffered from advanced breast cancer, so mother and daughter were accepted into a UN program that resettles people with serious medical issues. They went to Canada. The rest of the family, Sofiya's aunt, uncle, and cousins, were brought to the United States by a program that fast-tracks immigration by Christians in former Soviet Bloc countries. Unknown to both Canadian and US officials at the time, Sofiya was actually raised mostly by her aunt because her mother had been sick and was undergoing treatment on and off throughout most of Sofiya's life. When her mother finally succumbed to the disease late last year, Sofiya felt isolated in Canada. She was still a Ukrainian citizen. She applied for a visa to travel to the US but ultimately decided not to wait for it to come through. It would be a temporary travel visa if she got it, in any case. Her plan was to stay."

During the telling Agent Winton had switched from using "Ms. Makarenko" to "Sofiya," and I felt he had some sympathy for the young woman. He didn't glance at any notes. He knew her story.

"She decided not to wait. Contacts in the community put her in touch with Joe. She paid him everything she could put her hands on, almost twenty thousand dollars, to bring her into the US.

"We'd had our eyes on Joe for a long time. We believe he used to bring people in via a boat he owned to downeast Maine just over the border, and then overland from there. In the last couple of years that's been more difficult, and we picked up a few of his customers."

I nodded to show I understood. Regulations allowed the Border Patrol to put checkpoints up to a hundred miles from all land and coastal borders, which encompassed the entire state of Maine. They'd set up regularly on Route 95 in Penobscot County, snarling traffic and aggravating people just trying to get around. They also patrolled the bus stations and train stations.

"We knew Joe had switched to bringing people farther down the coast," Agent Winton continued. "Someone was meeting up with his boats at sea and taking his clients to Portland or even farther south. For a long time we had no suspicions as to whom. It's a big ocean.

"By that time, Special Agent Petrov had gone undercover as a part of Joe's demo crew. When they came back to Busman's Harbor for the third time in a year, we got very interested. It could have been that Mark Cochran was giving them lots of legitimate work, but Agent Petrov believed there was more to it.

"Once he got to the harbor, in what little spare time Joe gave him, Agent Petrov hung out at the marina looking for boat owners who might be working for Joe. It wasn't hard to spot Jason Caraway and his big boat. He didn't seem like much of a lobsterman. He came and went at strange hours. Often he appeared to have been away overnight. Based on the information Agent Petrov developed, we got a warrant and began looking into Caraway's finances."

"Did Jason know you were on to him?"

"Doubtful. We hadn't got far and we certainly hadn't brought him in for questioning," Winton said. "By that point we'd identified all the parts of the operation, Joe's contacts in Canada, Caraway the transport, and Joe himself and his crew, handling the financial transactions and the logistics, and taking the lion's share of the money."

"And then the storm came." I had figured that part out.

"Exactly. Terrible timing if ever there was—for us and for Sofiya Makarenko. Caraway set out to get her in fine weather. Even though the storm existed, it was predicted to pass much farther to the east when he left. But then it turned and headed straight for the Maine coast. Caraway realized he'd never make it farther south to whatever harbor town where they'd arranged to let Sofiya off. He headed to Morrow Island and left the girl there. Then he limped into Busman's Harbor, getting in at the last possible moment."

"Why did he leave her on the island?"

"We think he figured the marina would be bustling with people securing their boats before the storm and she'd certainly be seen. By the same token, he couldn't stay out on Morrow Island himself. As a divorced man, he was free to come and go, but with a major storm coming, someone was sure to check if he was okay, particularly if his boat was missing. They would probably raise the alarm and get out the Coast Guard, the last thing he wanted."

"I'm sure he wanted the *Money Honey* in a safe port as well," I said.

"Quite so." Winton shifted on the uncomfortable chairs.

"Jason's ex-wife, Pru, found a carryall with a woman's clothing in it aboard the *Money Honey* after the storm," I told the men. "She described the contents as 'intimate things.'"

"Probably whatever Sofiya could carry discreetly," Agent Winton said. "Where are these things now? There was nothing on Caraway's boat when we searched it after he was killed."

"Check with Pru Caraway," I told him. "It wouldn't surprise me if she chucked them into the harbor. She thought they belonged to someone Jason was sleeping with."

That almost brought a smile to Agent Winton's face, but he was exhausted and he'd lost a colleague. He went on. "We know from her writing in the journal, when the storm hit, it was terrifying for Sofiya. She took refuge in the hidden room. It was the only room that was furnished and the single, high window made her feel protected from the storm. Caraway hadn't left her with food or water and at the height of the storm she was afraid to go to look for any. She had no idea when or if he was coming back. She cried and prayed and wrote in the journal.

"When the storm cleared, she waited, but the seas were still high. She did find the pavilion and drank from the water cooler in the dining room. There wasn't any food around, only ingredients. She ate the packaged cookies in the gift shop, the ones shaped like lobsters."

"My mother thought the inventory was light. Where is Sofiya now?" I asked.

"We don't know. The ballpoint ran out of ink and she stopped recording what had happened."

"Did Joe kill Jason?"

Agent Winton ducked his head. "We believe so."

"Why?" I asked.

"Our working theory is Sofiya left the island somehow. Either she swam for it, or she was able to flag down a passing boat. We don't think she completed the journey with Caraway. We believe that nevertheless, Caraway demanded his cut from Joe. Caraway had gotten Sofiya into the US. He'd fulfilled his end of the bargain. A fight developed and Caraway threatened to inform on Joe, or something similar. It got him killed."

"What about Agent Petrov?" I asked.

"We believe he may have tried to intervene in Caraway's murder. As a law enforcement professional, he wouldn't have stood by while someone was murdered, no matter what they had done."

"Or," I said, "while bargaining for his life, Jason told Joe that Agent Petrov was law enforcement, and that's what got him killed."

"Why do you say that?" Winton was clearly surprised.

"They recognized each other at the clambake the day before the murder. I saw them exchange a look. Each was startled to see the other. I told Lieutenant Binder and Sergeant Flynn about it. I think, based on what you've told me, Jason had seen Agent Petrov at the marina, maybe even realized he was an agent. Jason was shocked when he saw him with Joe's crew, but probably thought the information might come in handy later."

"She did tell us about that look," Binder confirmed. "That could have been what happened."

"Why did they leave Jason's body under the wood-pile, but put Agent Petrov's in the channel?" I asked.

"We think they wanted Caraway's body to be found. As a member of the community, Jason would be missed. Joe had observed the fight between Jason and Terry Durand and he thought it might take us off the track." Winton cleared his throat. "Agent Petrov, on the other hand, they hoped we'd never find."

"So the dogs you brought to the island weren't look-ing for the murder weapon." I had figured that part out.

Winton shook his head. "Cadaver dogs. They didn't find him because he was in the water."

"Where are the Russians now?" I asked.

"They were gone from the island when we got there. The Coast Guard picked them up headed for the next peninsula. They weren't going to get very far very fast in the tub they were in."

"Was there a skinny, young guy with them?" I was almost afraid to ask.

"I don't have descriptions," Winton answered, "but there were five of them."

Thank goodness. "I believe the one named Alex

wasn't involved in any of it, not the human smuggling or the murders."

"We'll determine that." Agent Winton was all business.

I didn't know what would happen to Alex, but at least he was alive. "And Sofiya?" I asked.

"We don't know. She may be on the move. She may have drowned. If she shows up at her aunt's house, we'll be there." He paused. "We'll need you to come back in the morning to make a formal statement, about where you found the journal, how you spotted Agent Petrov's body, all of it." Winton stood. Our talk was at an end.

Flynn walked down the hallway and surprised me by giving me a hug before he sent me out into the night. "Take care of yourself," he said. "I called Chris to come and get you."

"I will." My throat closed and the emotions of the day flooded over me.

Chris was in his truck, waiting at the curb. He jumped out when he saw me and met me on the walk. I was in his arms before I started to cry.

Chapter Twenty-Five

Later that evening, Terry came up the stairs into our studio apartment. I was resting on the couch but I got up so we were all standing, awkwardly and spaced apart. Terry wore a wool red and black checked shirt as a jacket. I recognized it as an old one of Chris's.

Terry stared at his work boots. "Julia, I've come to say thank you. Lieutenant Binder has let me know Jason's death was related to something he was into that had nothing to do with me, or any old scores we had to settle, or with Emmy. Chris said you would help me and you did."

I was moved. This wasn't easy for him. "I'm not sure I did help. As you say, it had nothing to do with you."

"Chris told me you found the body and the notebook with the foreign writing. You had figured out enough of what was going on to know what the notebook meant. Don't say you did nothing. I owe you a lot. I want to do something for you. I don't have any money, but I can do you a favor. Name it."

My eyes met Chris's across the room. He gestured toward Terry. "This is between you and him."

"Thank you. I appreciate the offer very much," I said to Terry. "I give my favor to Chris."

They both laughed. "Oh, man," Terry said. "What does this mean? What do you want, little brother?"

The mood had lightened when they'd laughed but immediately turned serious again. Chris's face said he wasn't joking. "I want you to go to Emmy. I want you to compare your memories and determine if you could be Vanessa's father."

"What if she doesn't want to sit down with me, a guy she hardly knows, and compare our histories of nights barely remembered?"

"She'll do it," Chris said, "because you'll explain to her why it's important."

Terry's eyes widened. He knew what Chris meant.

"If it is possible," Chris continued, "if you could have crossed paths, I want you to take a paternity test, to be sure. And if you are Vanessa's father, I want you to take the Huntington's test and share the results with Emmy, so she knows. So she, and eventually Vanessa, can be prepared for the future."

"You haven't taken a test." Terry's temper flared and I thought for a moment he might back out of the whole thing.

"I'm not a father," Chris said quietly. "If I was, or if I thought I might become one"—he looked across the room at me—"I would take it in a heartbeat. I don't expect a cure in my lifetime. Maybe not even an effective treatment. If I've got it, I'll show symptoms soon. But Vanessa's eleven years old. You don't know what could happen. If a cure comes, she may not seek testing or treatment before it's too late if she has no idea she might have the gene."

Chris's logic was irrefutable. Terry, who had closed his arms over his chest when Chris started talking, dropped them to his sides. "Okay. I agree. I'll find Emmy and we'll have the conversation. But if I need to take the Huntington's test, I'm going to do it in Florida." The Huntington's test would take months. There was mandatory counseling before the test could be given and more before the results would be released.

"You're leaving town?" Chris hadn't expected it.

"If all this has taught me anything, it's there's nothing for me here," Terry said. "It's too complicated, too much history."

"I thought you were going to help me work on the cabin." Chris was plainly hurt.

"Better to get a clean start." Terry smiled. "Besides I think you might need the cabin soon." He looked around the studio and then at me. "This place might get too small. And it's time for me to see Mom. The last chance. Cherie's already there."

"You've talked to Cherie?" Chris was astonished.

"She wrote to me in prison, regular, and I wrote back. She moved down to help your dad five years ago. She visits Mom in the . . . place where she is."

"Last I heard she was in San Diego." Chris had been the one who stayed home, lost his chance at college so Cherie could finish high school. As far as he knew, she wasn't in touch with any of them. He didn't say it, but I could feel his pain. If she'd reached out, it should have been to him.

"Mom won't know you," Chris said. "She won't even know you're there."

Terry nodded to show he understood. "But I'll know I'm there. That's what's important."

Chapter Twenty-Six

Saturday morning, the family gathered at Mom's house to say good-bye to Marguerite and Tallulah. Chris would drive them to Portland to meet the train. Tallulah's husband, Jake, would meet them at North Station in Boston and see them home.

When Chris and I entered Mom's house, they were all in the dining room, including Livvie and Sonny, Page and Jack, Fee and Vee. I was surprised to see a stranger there, too. He was a robust man in his seventies with thick white hair and a deep tan. When he stood to greet us, he was tall, though narrow-shouldered with a bit of a gut. "Bill Beal," he said.

"Ah," I responded, understanding his presence. "Julia Snowden. This is my boyfriend, Chris Durand."

Chris gave me a puzzled look before he shook hands with Beal. With all the craziness of the previous day, I had forgotten to explain about him.

Beal sat back down and picked up the journal from the dining room table. "Lilly Smythe was my grandmother," he said.

"She married Captain Beal." Tallulah couldn't contain

herself long enough to let Bill Beal tell the story. "She didn't kill herself!"

"No. She married in 1898 and had four sons. The youngest was my father."

"Did you know about—?"

Beal turned the journal over in his hands. "No. Nothing." He paused. "I shouldn't say nothing. We knew my grandmother had worked on Morrow Island and my grandfather had captained for the Morrows and the island was where they fell in love. It was a romantic story in our family. Much later, after your family founded the clambake, and long after my grandparents were dead, we came over many times to celebrate birthdays, anniversaries, and such. We thought we were marking the occasions in a special spot, the beginning place for our family, so to speak. I don't think any of us, apart from my grandparents, knew what really happened."

"Did you know Lilly?" Livvie asked.

"Quite well. She died in 1968, the year I went off to college. She and my grandfather lived in the house at the head of the harbor, the white one where the Seafarer Inn is today. I grew up in town and spent every Thanksgiving, Christmas, and Easter there, and a lot of other days as well."

"Was she"—Livvie frowned, trying to find the right word—"happy?"

"I'm not sure 'happy' was a feature of that generation. They worked hard and made a life. My grandfather captained a fishing boat out of the harbor. It was hard, dirty work. He'd come home smelling of bait, hands rough from the sea with a thousand little cuts on them. My grandmother would make him shower in the basement and change his clothes before he could come upstairs.

"Their sons were born over twenty years. The oldest, Michael, was born in 1900, my dad in 1920. Michael fought in World War One and my dad in World War Two. They both made it home, thank goodness."

"Did she—" I tried to ask.

"Show any lasting trauma from the attempted rape?" Beal understood me. If "attempted" was even the right word. There might have been some things Lilly couldn't describe, even in her journal.

He shifted in his seat. "My grandmother was controlling. Everything had to be just so. Everyone had to behave according to a code that only she truly understood. In our immediate family, my mother, her daughter-in-law, bore the brunt of it. Nothing my mom did as a parent or housewife or townswoman was quite right."

"That's not the young woman in the journal," I said.

"No," Beal agreed. "It's not."

Perhaps having lost control of her life and her body on that terrible night had changed her forever.

"I didn't think anything of it," Beal continued. "To me, she was old-fashioned and not unlike most of my friends' grandmothers, though she was a little older. That generation had one code; we baby boomers had another. I loved her. My grandfather adored her."

That was something at least. Lilly had lived and she was loved. "And the sealed-off room?" I asked.

"Not a clue," Beal said. "To think it was sitting there all that time, even while my siblings, cousins, and I ate lobster dinners on your island."

"She left in a hurry," Tallulah pointed out. "Her personal things were left behind."

"The family story was that my grandfather sailed off

230   *Barbara Ross*

with her in the middle of the night so they could elope," Beal said. "Clearly there was more to the story."

"After she left, the family wouldn't have wanted to think about her," Marguerite said. "They may have pretended they didn't understand why she left so suddenly, but at least a few of them must have understood."

"To close the door to the room, even lock it, I get," Chris said. "But to seal it off, preserve it, hide it. It's extreme."

Marguerite cleared her throat. "My half brother Charles spent much more time at Windsholme than the rest of the family. William was based in New York, my mother and I in Boston. We would show up for the season, nothing more. When Charles was a young man, he oversaw the Morrow Ice operations on the Kennebec River. He lived in Bath and so had access to Windsholme in the spring and fall before the rest of the family arrived and after they left. He clearly had a crush on Lilly Smythe, and at an impressionable age he was a witness to what happened to her. Everyone has always said he was a sensitive soul. I would guess after Lilly left, the room was closed or even locked by the family, who didn't want to deal with it, and sometime later, after he was grown, Charles had the room sealed off."

We were all silent for a moment. "Sounds right," Bill Beal said. "As right as we can know."

"I've given the journal to Bill," Mom said.

"And I'll give it to the Busman's Harbor Historical Society once I've made copies for the family," Bill said.

Would Lilly have wanted that? Probably not. For her, it would be her greatest shame exposed, known to all her family, and available for anyone stopping at the historical society to read. But in a more enlightened age, we knew it wasn't her shame she described in the journal. It was someone else's.

"I'm sorry my uncle did that to your grandmother," Marguerite said, as if she'd been reading my mind.

"No need." Bill Beal stood and prepared to go. "I'm sorry to learn this about my grandmother and I am sure you were sorry to learn about your uncle, but it's in the past. Besides, if your family was in shipping in New England, as mine was, I'm sure they did worse things. Plenty of things to apologize for."

He was undoubtedly right.

He shook all our hands and said good-bye. Then Chris loaded Marguerite's and Tallulah's bags in his cab. They put on their coats and we all went out on the porch. There was a lot of kissing and hugging and promising to stay in touch. "Next summer!" Tallulah chirped.

"Yes," Mom said. "Bring your mother and Jake next time."

"You don't be strangers, either," Marguerite added. "We'll see you in Boston this winter."

We all promised that would be true, though as Chris pulled out of the driveway and headed down Main Street, I wondered. Marguerite was ninety-six. Though she seemed spry, any good-bye might be the last. At least she had lived a full life, more than full. Not like Jason. Not like Agent Petrov. And maybe not like Sofiya.

We waved until the cab was out of sight.

Chapter Twenty-Seven

Columbus Day was beautiful. The sun shone bright, though there was that crispness in the air that announced unmistakably, "fall." We hadn't been able to hold the clambake on Saturday or Sunday because there were still law enforcement personnel on the island. But for the last day of the season, we were back.

Mom was in the gift shop, conducting a 50 percent off sale. "Everything must go!" But everything wouldn't. Whatever was left would be boxed in our plastic containers and stored in the house by the dock until the next summer.

Chris was giving Sonny a hand at the clambake fire. There were only two of them and we had a full load of customers, people who'd planned to come on the last day, and those who had missed out because they'd had to cancel the two days before. I watched Sonny and Chris hustle to cover the piled seafood with the saltwater-soaked tarps. Chris's movements were strong and graceful as he flung the heavy cloth. I loved watching him when he was unaware. My body vibrated in a rhythm that felt like it matched his. Would he always be graceful, or would he soon experience the tremors and ticks that marked the onset of symptoms of Huntington's? If he did, how would he cope? How would I?

Terry had left that morning on the beginning of his trip to Florida, a bus ride to Portland, another to Boston, and then a flight. Chris had given him the money. A loan, they'd both called it. "Until I can get on my feet," Terry said. He'd met the night before with Emmy after she got off her shift at Crowley's. She'd agreed to talk to him and share their mutual history after he showed her a snapshot Chris had found of his mother when she was Vanessa's age. The likeness was haunting, and I imagined for Emmy even more so when Terry told her that his mother was in a nursing home, unable to control her mind or her body and sure to die soon from an inherited disease. Emmy had agreed to a paternity test for Vanessa. They'd take it from there.

For now, Emmy scurried about, readying her tables for the meal. Vanessa and Page chased Luther around the lawn as he laughed and shrieked. Jack, frustrated, rose to his knees and tried to crawl after them, but he couldn't quite manage it. He cried in frustration until Page picked him up and ran with him in her arms. "Careful, girls!" Emmy called.

I had worried that when Terry left Chris would feel like he'd failed. He'd wanted a relationship, for them to spend time together. He'd been forthright with me about how painful it was to discover Cherie was in touch with Terry and their father, but not with him. Nonetheless, as the days got shorter and cooler, and the countdown to opening our restaurant marched forward, Chris smiled and joked more. He'd always had a sense of humor and a gentling teasing way with me, but he seemed lighter and happier than in any of our time together, as if another weight, or a part of a weight, had been lifted. In a moment of weakness he'd agreed to take part in a skit for a haunted house tour Busman's Harbor was running for Halloween. I could even believe he was looking forward to it.

Windsholme was to be boarded up for the winter. Mark Cochran would find another demolition team in the spring.

The mansion had added another ghost—Special Agent Petrov. His body had gone home to his parents and I was glad he would rest among people who knew who he really was.

The harbor seal was gone, too. I hoped, like Lilly Smythe, he had found his way back to where he was supposed to be.

Recipes

Greek Style Lamb Chops Sous Vide

Because the title of the book is Sealed Off, *I thought it would be clever to include a sous vide recipe, since food cooked sous vide is sealed in a plastic bag. Get it? The question was who should cook it? The answer had to be Julia's sister, Livvie, and her husband, Sonny. Livvie is an accomplished cook and Sonny is the grill master, though Chris might have been an equally good choice as the chef. My husband developed this absolutely delicious recipe.*

Ingredients

4 thick-cut lamb chops (rib chops—1½ to 2 inches, or shoulder chops—1 to 1½ inches)
Olive oil for rubbing chops and drizzling
Salt
Black pepper
2 large cloves garlic, chopped
16 sprigs fresh oregano
16 sprigs fresh marjoram
8 thinly cut slices of lemon
2 1-gallon size or 4 1-quart size sealable food storage bags or vacuum sealer bags

Instructions

Keep chops refrigerated until ready to use; some people even like to freeze for 20 minutes before beginning.

Set up your sous vide unit according to manufacturer instructions and preheat water bath to 134 degrees.

Rub the chops all over with olive oil. Generously salt and pepper on both sides.

Preheat a gas grill on high for at least 10 minutes or heat a heavy-bottomed fry pan on high, then add a Tablespoon of olive oil until it begins to smoke.

Sear the chops 1 minute on each side and set aside to cool briefly.

When ready to handle, drizzle chops on one side with olive oil and sprinkle with some garlic. Repeat on other side of chops.

Place chops in bags.

Put 2 sprigs of oregano and marjoram on each side of chop. Add 1 slice of lemon to each side.

Vacuum seal bags or, if using food storage bags, seal ¾ of the way across the top and slide gently into the water bath, allowing the water to push out the air, and then completely seal to prevent water seeping inside.

Cook for 2 hours.

15 minutes before serving, preheat grill or fry pan again. Remove chops from bag, discarding herbs and lemon. Sear chops for 1 minute on each side. Set on a platter and allow to rest for 10 minutes.

Serves 4

Halibut Pizzaiola

Fee Snugg, another great cook in the series, makes the halibut pizzaiola in the book. She, Livvie, and Chris have gotten into quite a little cooking competition, and all the Snowden clan are the beneficiaries.

Ingredients

3 Tablespoons olive oil, divided
2 6-ounce filets halibut
1/8 teaspoon red pepper flakes (optional)
2 anchovy filets, chopped (optional)
1 large clove garlic, chopped
1 teaspoon dried oregano
1 28-ounce can ground peeled tomatoes

Instructions

Heat 1 Tablespoon of olive oil in a sauté pan over high heat. Season the halibut filets with salt and pepper and sear 1 minute on each side. Remove from pan and set aside.

Turn the burner to medium, and using the same pan, add the remaining olive oil and red pepper flakes, if using. Add the anchovy, if using, and stir, crushing, with a wooden spoon until the anchovy melts into the oil. Add the garlic and oregano and stir together for 2 minutes. Add the tomato, season with salt and pepper, and bring to a boil. Simmer for 15 minutes. Add the halibut and cook for 8 to 10 minutes. Plate the halibut, spooning some of the sauce over the top.

Serves 2

Slow Cooker Cioppino

This recipe wasn't meant to be in the book. My husband Bill made it for me and I decided it had to be. It's an East Coast take on a West Coast dish. I gave this one to Chris to make for Julia's family. The comforting food expresses the comfort he's found with them.

Ingredients

2 medium onions, chopped
1 cup celery, chopped
3 large cloves garlic, chopped
1 28-ounce can diced tomatoes
4 cups seafood stock
½ cup white wine
1 6-ounce can tomato paste
6 sprigs of fresh thyme
4 sprigs of fresh oregano
2 bay leaves
2 teaspoons kosher salt
¼ teaspoon red pepper flakes
¼ teaspoon ground black pepper
1 or 2 cooked lobster bodies (no tails, no claws, heads removed)
1½ pounds flaky white fish like haddock or cod, cut into 1-inch pieces
1½ pounds shrimp, peeled and deveined
2 6-ounce cans chopped clams with their juice
8 ounces lump crabmeat
8 ounces cooked lobster meat

Instructions

Stir together onions, celery, garlic, tomatoes, stock, wine, and tomato paste, herbs, and seasonings in slow cooker pot. Add lobster bodies. Set to high and cook for 4 hours. Remove lobster bodies, herb sprigs, and bay leaves. Add fish and cook on low for 30 minutes longer. Serve with crusty bread.

Serves 8

Olga's Brownies

My mother-in-law used to make these brownies for her young family, and they are the first thing my husband recalls making by himself. Over the years the recipe fell out of use in the family and we thought it was lost. Bill searched the Internet to no avail. After his mom died, we found the recipe among her effects and Bill has shared it with his siblings. In Sealed Off, *Vee makes the brownies and brings them to dinner at the Snowdens', which is entirely appropriate because, like Vee, my mother-in-law ran a B and B in Maine and was an excellent cook and baker.*

Ingredients

1 cup butter
1 cup cocoa
2 cups sugar
5 eggs
3 teaspoons vanilla
1½ cups flour
½ teaspoon baking powder
¾ teaspoon salt
1 cup chopped nuts (optional)
1 Tablespoon cooking oil of your choice to grease the pan

Instructions

Preheat oven to 350 degrees. In a large saucepan, melt butter. Remove from heat. Stir in cocoa until it mixes completely, then stir in sugar until it mixes completely. Add the 5 eggs one at a time, stirring each in before you add the next. Add the vanilla, flour, baking powder and salt, stirring each one before adding the next. Stir in the nuts, if desired.

Bake for 30 to 35 minutes in a greased, 9" x 13" pan. Serves 15 to 20

Ma's Pot Roast

In Sealed Off *I attribute Jacqueline's pot roast recipe to a German housekeeper who helped raise her. In reality it was one of my maternal grandmother, Ethel McKim's, best dishes, often served on the first day of an extended visit to my grandparents' home on the Jersey shore. She always said, "It's better the second day."*

Ingredients

3 pounds beef rump
2 large onions, cut up
2 Tablespoons catsup
2 Tablespoons apple cider vinegar
1 teaspoon sugar
6 drops Worcestershire sauce
Salt and pepper to taste
Flour to thicken gravy

Instructions

Preheat oven to 300 degrees. On stove, brown meat on all sides in an oven-ready pan. Add remaining ingredients. Add water to come halfway up the side of the meat.

Bake for 3 hours until meat is soft.

Remove meat from pan. Skim fat off gravy and thicken with flour.

Hint: Prepare the day before serving. Take meat out of gravy and wrap in foil. Pour gravy in bowl. Refrigerate overnight. On day of serving, slice meat and place in an 8" x 8" baking dish, cover with gravy, and heat in oven at 350 degrees for 30 minutes.

Serves 4 to 6

ACKNOWLEDGMENTS

I would like to thank my granddaughter Viola Jane Carito for helping me with the seal research for this book. Together we read (many, many times) *André, The Famous Harbor Seal* (by Fran Hodgkins, illustrated by Yetti Frenkel, Down East Books, 2003), *Do Seals Ever . . . ?* (by Fran Hodgkins, illustrated by Marjorie Leggitt, Down East Books, 2017), and our favorite, *Cecily's Summer* (by Nan Lincoln, illustrated by Patricia J. Wynne, Bunker Hill, 2005). I also read the books for grown-ups, *The Summer of Cecily* (by Nan Lincoln, Bunker Hill, 2004) and *A Seal Called Andre* (by Harry Goodridge and Lew Dietz, Dea, 2014). The days are long past when a civilian could have a harbor seal as a pet as Harry Goodridge did, or even foster an orphan pup as Nan Lincoln did, and for good reasons. Nonetheless their books provide wonderful, intimate portraits of these smart sea mammals.

I loved the book *The Big House: A Century in the Life of an American Summer Home* (by George Howe Colt, Scribner, 2003) for the glimpse of generations of a family occupying the same old summer place. Thanks especially for giving me the image of Marguerite Morales's reaction to the place she knew in childhood rendered in two-dimensional floor plans.

I would like to thank my sailing neighbors, Jack and Zdenka Griswold, for helping me figure out how long it would take the Morrow yacht to get from Boston to Busman's Harbor in 1898, and what tasks Terry Durand might do aboard the *Dark Lady* to repay his brother, Chris, for the temporary housing.

Bruce Robert Coffin took time out from writing his own Detective Byron Mystery series to help me understand what Terry Durand would have been charged with for the shooting at Hudson's and how much prison time he might have served.

Thank you to Jessica Ellicott, who endured a marathon video session while we plotted the mystery. And thanks to Sherry Harris, who reviewed the manuscript and gave me many helpful comments even while serving as the busy president of the National Board of Sisters in Crime.

Thanks to everyone at Kensington Publishing. I always appreciate your flexibility and willingness to try new things in the face of a changing market. I would like to especially acknowledge my editor, John Scognamiglio, and my publicist, Larissa Ackerman. I'd also like to thank my agent, John Talbot.

To my Wicked blogmates, Maddy Day, Jessica Ellicott, Sherry Harris, Julia Henry, and Liz Mugavero, I couldn't do this without you.

Special thanks this year to my Portland, Maine, crime-writing community. Your embrace of Bill and me since we moved to Portland has made this major life change so much easier and even more wonderful. Thank you Brenda Buchanan, Richard J. Cass, Bruce Robert Coffin, Chris Holm, Gayle Lynds, and Joseph Souza, and all your amazing spouses.

Thank you, as ever, to my husband, Bill Carito. Bill develops almost all the recipes for the Maine Clambake Mysteries, in this case donating his work to Livvie, Fee, and Chris. He has been so insanely patient and supportive this year while I slipped in an extra book, *Jane Darrowfield, Professional Busybody,* and an extra novella, "Hallowed Out" for *Haunted House Murder* (both from Kensington). I cannot, truly, express my gratitude and love.

And to my family, who arrived en masse to visit us in Key West on the day I turned in this manuscript, I love you all, Bill Carito, Rob, Sunny, and Viola Carito, and Kate, Luke, and Etta Donius, our newest addition.

Connect with

Visit us online at
KensingtonBooks.com
to read more from your favorite authors, see books
by series, view reading group guides, and more.

for sneak peeks, chances to win books and prize packs,
and to share your thoughts with other readers.

facebook.com/kensingtonpublishing
twitter.com/kensingtonbooks

Tell us what you think!

To share your thoughts, submit a review,
or sign up for our eNewsletters, please visit:
KensingtonBooks.com/TellUs.

Catering and Capers with
Isis Crawford!

Grab These Cozy Mysteries
from
Kensington Books

Follow P.I. Savannah Reid
with
G.A. McKevett